CLOSE TO DEATH

CLOSE
TO DEATH

JOHN CROWE

A BUENA COSTA COUNTY MYSTERY

DODD, MEAD & COMPANY · NEW YORK

1 2 3 4 5 6 7 8 9 10

Library of Congress Cataloging in Publication Data

_____

   Close to death.

   (His A Buena Costa County mystery)
   I. Title.
PZ4.L9892Cl [PS3562.Y44] 813'.5'4 79-1213
ISBN 0-396-07675-0

To Jo and Bob Gottsdanker,
for wine, song and criticism

1

The difference between a dream and a nightmare is as thin as a human hair. Balanced on a knife-edge. And moved by something as insignificant as a pebble falling into the sea, the dream can slide unseen into the darkness of nightmare.

It was a clear, cool evening in March when John Perkins stopped his car at the side of the back highway on the outskirts of Fremont, California. The end of a day as close to spring as it ever got in Buena Costa County, and Perkins stopped on the road because he was excited. He had suddenly seen a dream become a possibility.

A free-lance architect and lecturer in architecture at Fremont State University, Perkins had wanted to design and build his own house for a long time. A house that would perfectly fit the life-style of his wife and himself, the way he wanted it and where he wanted it. And where he wanted it was near Fremont on a spot with a wide view of the sea. The problem was money—lots with views aren't cheap in Southern California, and a thirty-year-old free-lance architect is rarely rich, even when his wife also works, so the dream house remained a dream until that day in March.

1

Perkins had driven from the university along the back highway many times without really seeing the "For Sale" sign on a narrow lot perched on a knoll directly above the highway. Perhaps it was the sense of spring, but this time he saw it and stopped. He climbed to the top of the knoll.

The view was to the west, wide and vast across the city and the sweep of the sea. The lot itself was part of Mar Vista Estates, with two ranch-style houses close by, and many more all across the rolling rural development. On the very edge of Mar Vista, and not really a lot at all. A forty-five-foot-wide splinter of a lot left when an access road had been built to the highway for the growing population of Mar Vista Estates.

Perkins walked all around the narrow patch of weed-grown land. Designing a house that would conform to county residential setback regulations and still be liveable and what he wanted would take some doing. A challenge to the architect in him. More important, there was no way an ordinary house could be built on the lot, and it was very close to the highway, so few people, if any, would want to buy it. That should make it inexpensive, even cheap.

His excitement growing, a design and floor plan already forming in his mind, he drove home to tell his wife the news.

*

The office of Hansen Realty was a stucco bungalow on a Fremont side street. Phil Hansen was exuberant that April afternoon.

"Signed and sealed, Barb! Five thousand, but I never really thought I'd ever sell that little lemon of a lot."

"What can he build on it?" Barbara Stewart wondered.

"Who cares? A cottage or something."

"Isn't there a covenant in Mar Vista?"

"The Architectural Control Committee? Hell, it's never

even met. I don't think there is a committee anymore. Two of the members quit years ago."

"Perhaps Perkins should talk with Gordon or another lawyer, just to be sure."

"Forget Perkins, and forget your husband." Hansen grinned.

He went to her. A broad-shouldered, athletic-looking man in his early forties, handsome and with thick, dark hair, he was only a few inches taller than she was. He kissed her.

"Let's celebrate. Right now."

"Stop it, Phil!" But she let him kiss her again.

*

By late April John Perkins had his design ready for the builder. He spread the drawing and the plans out on the kitchen table of their rented house for his wife to look at.

"See, it will be two cubes, each two-storys high, with a one-story connecting entrance hall. The whole house just thirteen feet wide to take care of the setback regulations, and seventy-eight feet long to fit nicely on the lot."

"You've got our black-and-white tile floor in the hall, and a brick floor in the kitchen," Cathy Perkins said. "John, it's beautiful."

"Two spiral staircases, the one picture window in the living room for the view, and just narrow slit windows everywhere else for privacy. The whole back wall for hanging our paintings."

"No one will be able to tell when we're home or not," Cathy said. "But, can we really afford it?"

"Barely," Perkins grinned. "I give the go-ahead tomorrow."

*

Maxwell Bowman stood in the shade of his carport and stared at the seventy-eight-foot-long blank wall of rough

3

reddish wood not thirty feet away. A small white-haired old man, Bowman turned to look at his own barn-red and white-trimmed ranch house on its immaculate lawn bordered by his wife's neat flower beds. Then he walked across his side lawn and around to the front of the new house where John Perkins was supervising the unloading of furniture from the moving van.

"Too hot even for August," Bowman said. "Moving in kind of fast, aren't you, Perkins? Kind of early?"

"My wife couldn't wait. She's bought a brand new outfit for the housewarming. We'll landscape later, finish the trim."

"You're really going to live in that thing?"

"Yes," Perkins said, "we are."

"It's a goddamn eyesore, Perkins!"

"That's a matter of opinion, Bowman."

"It's not even a house! You can't call that thing a house! I'm damned if I know what you could call it!"

"I'm sorry you feel that way."

"Where'd you pick up all the junk you used to build it? That lousy siding looks inferior to me."

"Sorry, it's perfectly up to code. Cedar veneer. It'll weather to a nice warm brown."

"One window in the whole damned tomb? No windows at all on my side? What the hell are you planning to do in there?"

"My wife and I both work all day, Bowman. At night we like to read or entertain—in private. The back wall is for our art collection. Our needs are different from yours."

"Then take your crazy needs somewhere else! That thing is an insult to Mar Vista! It'll ruin the whole neighborhood."

"If you give it a chance, let it weather and grow into the landscaping, I think you'll find that it will blend right into

4

the land, become part of the natural scene."

"Is that damned wall going to become invisible? Two orange crates would look better! Brown or goddamn pink, that wall is still nothing but a wall, and it ruins my property!"

"I'm sorry you don't like it. We do."

*

Cathy Perkins said, "I'm scared, John."

Perkins stirred the ice in his martini. Outside, through the single picture window, the late-evening September twilight glowed over the city below and the sea. In the warm, silent new house the light was soft and the clink of the ice echoed like small bells in the comfortable sunken living room.

"Our whole savings are in this house," Cathy said.

"Not to mention a mortgage to choke an elephant."

"Can they make us tear it down, John?"

Her face seemed close to tears. A young face, she wasn't yet thirty, round and girlish, with a small nose and full cheeks. A small mouth over slightly visible teeth, and dark brown eyes. Her body as round and girlish as her face, five-feet-five, her hands twisting together.

"I hope not, Cath," Perkins said. "They haven't had much luck with that Architectural Control Committee. As Hansen told us, it doesn't seem to exist, they can't even locate the one member who didn't quit because they never met. The lawyer Hansen got us, Gordon Stewart, says that if they take it to court we'll countersue. He thinks we've got a good chance to win."

"A chance?" Cathy said. "That's all? Just a chance?"

"A *good* chance. We can appeal at every step. We'll fight it all the way."

"As long as our money lasts."

Perkins said nothing. He drank his martini in the silent dream house.

*

There were seventeen members of the Mar Vista Civic Association in the big living room of builder and Association president George Spira. An angry chorus behind spokesmen Maxwell Bowman and Colonel Benjamin Hillock, U.S. Army (Ret.).

"Bowman and I are the closest to that monstrosity," Colonel Hillock pointed out, "but when it ruins property values, Spira, and it will, you'll lose more than any of us."

An imposing man, tall and lean and erect, Hillock paced the room angrily in front of the silent Spira. Except for a gray mustache and almost totally bald head, the colonel could have passed for a man fifteen years younger than sixty-two.

"How do you think you're going to sell the rest of your Mar Vista houses at a decent price when the first thing people see are those damned cubes?" Maxwell Bowman said. "You'll lose money, if you can sell them at all."

"I'll protect my interests," George Spira said, "one way or another. The question is how?"

In a brocade armchair, Spira looked less at home in his big house than any of them. A widower in his fifties, Spira had begun as a construction worker in northern California, and he looked it. Stocky and rough in a green corduroy suit, the builder still had the weathered face and hands of a workingman.

"The Architectural Control Committee is a washout," he said. "There isn't any committee. You haven't scared Perkins out of that house, and lawyers cost money. What about a compromise?"

"What compromise?" Colonel Hillock said. "What the hell can be done to those boxes except tear them down?"

"Perkins won't compromise," Maxwell Bowman said. "He's an architect. I think he built that house to challenge the town, push his crazy ideas against good, normal homes.''

"Those university people are all radicals!'' someone said.

"They better keep their ideas out of our neighborhood!''

"You don't have to look at that thing every day!''

Spira listened to the angry chorus.

"Okay, we go to court. You better all be ready for a fight. Perkins has hired Gordon Stewart, he's sure to counter-sue.'' Spira watched them all. "The people in Mar Vista will back us, but not everyone else will. It could split the community, get nasty. And this is an election year.''

*

Attorney Gordon Stewart was a tall, thin, quiet man who had been losing his lank blond hair for years but still played tennis every day. He always ate lunch in a cafeteria around the corner from his office, alone and usually working. When he returned to his second-floor office on a sunny late September day, his secretary told him George Spira was waiting.

"Sparring's over. Complaint, motions, subpoenas, demurrers, praecipes. Tell Perkins he can't win in court.''

"I'm not sure that he can't.''

"We don't have the Committee, but we've got the covenant.''

"Then we'll have to challenge the covenant.''

"That means all covenants in all developments. It'll split the community, Gordon. Wide open! You'll be on the wrong side.''

"Which side is the right side, George?''

"Your side and mine! The solid side, the business side.'' Spira walked the office. "Lose in court, and Perkins loses it all. The house ordered torn down, swept away.''

"You have something in mind?''

"Let Perkins tear the house down on his own. I'll get the Mar Vista people to contribute enough to let him build a regular house, or to sell the lot and come out about even."

"Meaning you'd 'contribute' most of it. It's that vital?"

"I don't want the community ripped up! Not with elections a month off. I want Tucker to win. It's important, Gordon."

"For the community, or for you?"

"Will you get Perkins to tear it down?"

"It's important that a man has the right to build any house he wants anywhere he wants in this country and in this county."

"A crusade? Is Perkins worth it, Gordon? Is it a matter of principle to him?"

"Does that mean something?"

"It means I won't let us all be used, you understand?"

Alone in his office, Gordon Stewart sat turning a pencil in his hands. His wife came in. She walked past his desk to the window above the side street.

"I saw George Spira leave."

"Made an offer about the Perkins mess. Or I think he did."

"Did you take the offer? If he made it."

"Did you want me to?"

Barbara Stewart remained at the window for a time. Then she turned and sat down across the office facing her husband. So slender at five-feet-eight she was almost angular, she wore a navy blue suit with a tight jacket and a loose skirt that framed very good legs. The legs and her soft, high-boned face were heavily tanned, and with her shoulder-length blond hair gave little hint of her forty-five years.

"You'll go to court then?"

"Unless the Mar Vista people change their minds,"

8

Stewart said. "Why do you care, Barb? You didn't sell that lot, Phil Hansen did. You have no connection."

"Phil sold the lot."

Her blue eyes seemed to be turned inward.

"You want me to stay out of court, make my client accept a compromise for Hansen's sake?"

"Does that make you angry? Make you hate me?"

"Would it matter much? Do you really care, Barbara?"

"I care," she said. "I don't know if it matters."

"I don't want you hurt by Hansen, or by anyone else."

"So you've heard that Tom McKay is back in town?"

"Yes."

She sat silently swinging her leg, distracted.

"Bill's in Fremont too," Stewart said.

"Here?" Her inward eyes darkened. "Why?"

"It seems that Senator Eller sent him down to work on the election."

"I don't want him here, Gordon!"

"He's your son, Barbara. You'll have to tell him."

She got up abruptly and walked to the door. She didn't open the door.

"Then you won't tell Perkins to settle it before everything gets worse? At least compromise? Privately."

"No."

"No," she said. "I always admired that about you, didn't I? So firm in your work. I always liked that."

2

At eleven-thirty on the first Monday in October, Cathy Perkins took a report she had finished editing to her boss and told him she would leave early for lunch. The offices of Ocean Sciences, Inc., were on the eastern outskirts of Fremont, and when Cathy drove out of the parking lot she turned east.

She drove to a Bonanza Steak House in a shopping center on the highway to San Vicente. She did not see the car that followed her from her offices. A small orange Nova.

In the restaurant she sat down in a booth where a quick-eyed young man in jeans and a denim jacket was drinking a beer. Cathy ordered a martini.

"Well?" the young man said.

"We go to trial next week."

She did not look at the young man, watched the waiter as he set down her martini.

"I know," the young man said. "They want blood. Tear it down. No tolerance, no compromise."

"Mr. Spira, the developer, told our lawyer that if we tore it down ourselves, dropped our countersuit, the Mar Vista

Association would try to raise enough money so we could build a normal house or sell the lot and go somewhere else. Or almost enough money."

"They're all heart. Under the table, nothing in writing, and you probably take a good loss even if they come through at all! What did lawyer Stewart say about that?"

"He said no, and so did my husband. He wants to fight."

"Win or lose," the young man said. "Going into court is always a risk."

He smiled. Cathy looked at him now.

"So?" he said. "Are we in business?"

Cathy finished her martini. She glanced nervously around the crowded lunchtime restaurant. She nodded.

"Then I better get to work. You have some lunch to give me a start, just in case."

Alone, Cathy Perkins had another martini before she finally ordered lunch. As she ate she continued to look around the big room full of diners, but she didn't notice the small, muscular man with the heavy black mustache who watched from a rear table.

*

Mrs. Estelle Bowman drew on her white gloves. On her way out of the house she glanced into the study where the men were.

"I'll be home by five, Maxwell."

Bowman stood. "Come in, Estelle. We're discussing the Perkins house again."

"It's Monday, dear, my garden club."

Through the study window, Maxwell Bowman watched her walk to the car, thick and slow in her pale blue dress, a white hat perched on her gray hair. He saw her look toward the blank cedar wall that seemed to menace their own house, and look quickly away. She got into the car, drove off.

11

"His dream house," Bowman said. "What about our dream house!"

Seated behind him, Colonel Benjamin Hillock shook his head.

"It's a damned crime," Hillock said.

Phil Hansen was on the leather couch. "If I'd known what they planned, I'd never have sold them the lot."

Bowman turned. "You'd sell your mother's grave for a hot dog stand! Why didn't you warn them about the covenant?"

"I did!"

"And told them not to worry about it! No one had ever enforced it! I've seen their countersuit!"

Colonel Hillock said, "We're not here to fight each other, are we? Is there anything we can come up with without going to court? I'm damned if I want to spend my money, wait perhaps a year or more, when it's Perkins who should be paying."

"Spira warned us, and we agreed to do it," Bowman said.

"He might agree to modify the house," Hansen said, "if we had a design. Put in windows, maybe a porch and a peaked shake roof. Paint it white, landscape heavily, and it wouldn't look that different from an ordinary two-story house."

"You think that's possible?" Hillock said.

"Perkins would never agree," Bowman said.

Hansen said, "Why not buy it, then? Make those modifications yourselves, and sell it again. I'd buy it for you, but I just don't have the cash right now."

"That's not much different from the offer Spira made," Hillock said. "Why would he take it?"

"Offer a good price. A decent profit."

"I'm damned if I'll give that man a profit!" Bowman

12

raged. "That would be simple blackmail! Maybe what he really wants!"

"In court you could lose," Hansen said.

"He's right, Bowman," Hillock said.

"No," Bowman said. "We'll get rid of that house and those people one way or another. They won't win."

*

The small, muscular man with the heavy black mustache sat down on Gordon Stewart's office couch. Casual and relaxed, he leaned back on the couch with his hands in the pockets of his gray slacks, his legs stretched out. Stewart was at his desk.

"Have you seen your mother?" the lawyer said.

"Not yet. Work before pleasure."

"You're not going to stay at the house?"

"When Grace and the kids come down in a few days. Still defending subversives and troublemakers, aren't you?"

The muscular man smiled. With his bristling mustache he could have been a self-assured businessman in his forties. But when he smiled, up close, there was a young face under the mustache, and his self-assurance took on a touch of arrogance.

"And you still work for reactionaries who think that the right to keep anything you steal fair and square is the American way."

"It's what everyone really thinks! Senator Eller's going to be attorney general and governor. The voters are waking up to bleeding hearts like Charley Tucker. He bails criminals out, Eller puts them in!"

"Eller and you. But he must be nervous about Buena Costa County to send his favorite hatchet man down."

"We'll find a good issue to work with."

Stewart shook his head. "Father and son. I wonder if

13

we'll ever agree on anything, Bill? From dogs to doughnuts.''

"You're not my father, Gordon."

"No," Stewart agreed. "He's back in Fremont, did you know? On his boat at the marina."

"He's not my father either."

"You can't change that by spelling your name differently. Bill Mackay is still Tom McKay's son."

"No he isn't," Bill Mackay said. He stretched on the couch, studied Stewart. "You're going to take this Perkins thing all the way? Tear down the community, push radical ideas? Defend destroyers of our standards instead of the builders?"

"One of your Sacramento speeches? Is the Perkins house the good issue you're going to work for Eller with?"

"That depends on Tucker. We know where our voters will stand, eh? Tucker can lose a lot of votes whichever side he takes, or maybe if he takes no side."

"I'm sorry. A man has the right to build his own house."

"Theory. Fuzzy-headed and empty."

"But the truth."

"The truth is what the majority says it is," Bill Mackay said. He sat up on the couch. "You think these Perkinses are as pure as you?"

"I hope so."

"You should hope less, find out more," Bill Mackay said. "And I should let you hang yourself, but I'll help you out. I think the Perkinses are up to something, have some angle. I think there's more than a dream house in this. For them, or for someone else." He stood up, went to the door. "You could get hung out on a dirty limb, you know? Tell Mother I might see her later."

*

Burly, balding, in his early sixties and burned black by seventeen thousand miles of sea and sun, Tom McKay was

14

sweating in the October sun of the Fremont marina as he chipped paint from the foredeck of his forty-foot sloop *Paloma*. He looked up as he felt the boat heel and sway.

"Well, Barbara! How are you?"

Barbara Stewart leaned on the sloop rail. She smiled down at McKay. She stopped smiling and looked out across the marina and its rows of masts like the ranked spears of some savage army toward the breakwater and the open sea beyond.

"It's been a long time," she said.

"Five years," McKay said. "I sailed half around the world, Barb—Tahiti, Bora Bora, Samoa, the Marquesas. Seventeen hundred miles. I've had drinks at Quinn's Bar in Papeete, lived with the natives in Samoa, painted in the Marquesas."

"I meant us. A lot more than five years for us. Since we talked." She continued to stare out to sea. "Tahiti? The Marquesas? It sounds wonderful. I wish I could have been there."

"You rejected my ways of life a long time ago."

"A long time ago."

McKay stood up. He wiped his hands on a cloth that hung from his belt. He wore nothing but ragged cut-off shorts and deck shoes.

"Is something wrong, Barbara?"

"What?"

"You just came to welcome me back?"

Her eyes turned away from the sea. She looked around the sea-worn sloop as if she hadn't really seen where she was before. "Bill's in town."

"Our ideal of a Hitler Youth?"

"He's an animal!"

"I wouldn't know, would I? You took him away from me twenty years ago."

"I'm sorry." She looked back toward the sea.

15

"Twenty-two years," McKay said. "He was three, so now he's twenty-five. Still calls himself Mackay instead of McKay?"

She sat down on the peeling deckhouse, turned to look toward the beach and the city in the October afternoon.

"You picked a bad time, I'm sorry." She appeared to look for something in the city. "I seem to be sorry about a great deal. Today."

"Bad time because Bill's in town? Tell him to stay away."

"I haven't seen him." She shook her head. "This cube house affair."

"Your real estate work?"

"Yes. No. It's not mine, Phil Hansen's. No, not even his. He only sold the lot. No way of knowing."

"Your work's going well? With Hansen?"

She watched the water lapping at the sloop. "I can't be close to him, Tom. I never could, could I? Be close?"

"To Hansen?"

"I tried hard, Tom. To be close to Gordon. The way he wanted it. I admire him, I really do. He's going to defend that awful house. But he's right, I know that. He's the one who's right, clean. We're wrong."

"Stewart always had principles."

She said, "Was I a very bad wife?"

"You mean to me? You think I still think about it?" McKay turned away from her, bent leaning on the rail. "You were a young wife, maybe too young. You said I was a bad husband."

"Did I?"

"I wish you had been with me out there in the islands. You'd have liked it. The sun, no pressures."

"I've failed Gordon. I failed you. Everyone."

16

"I'm going back. Out there. Maybe around the world."

"It's going to ruin us. This house thing. All of us. Gordon and me. If only he wouldn't let it go on."

"I can handle any ship now, anywhere. An old salt. We could see all the other islands I've never seen. Fiji. Micronesia. Go to Australia, maybe down to the ice."

She stood up.

"You'll talk to him at least, Tom? Bill."

"I doubt if he'll want to talk to me, Barbara."

"See him. Please?"

McKay shook his head. "A Gestapo man. Not my son."

She walked to the gangplank and climbed to the dock. McKay's wind-creased eyes watched her disappear into the marina parking lot.

*

The motel room was less than a mile from the Fremont marina. Maxwell Bowman came in. He was nervous.

"Well," he said, "did you see your father?"

"Stepfather," Bill Mackay said. "I saw him."

"And?"

"I put on some pressure. He'll think about it."

"But he's not backing off yet?" Bowman sat down, ran a thin hand through his white hair. "Goddamned lawyers."

"If I can't get it done you don't pay me. I'll get it done." Mackay reached under his jacket and dropped a Colt .357 magnum revolver on the desk. Bowman flinched. Mackay smiled. "I'm a licensed bodyguard for Senator Eller."

"Violence is—"

"Is sometimes all we've got left to stop the enemy," Mackay said. "But don't worry, egghead radicals like Perkins and my stepfather are cowards. Tricky talk and subversion, that's their style. I might show them the iron, but I've got other ideas too. I'll keep on pressuring my step-

17

father and watching the Perkinses. Especially the woman. She's got something going on I don't think she wants anyone to know about. It might be something that'll hang them in court, make them drop the whole thing if we dig it out."

"All right," Bowman said. "I don't care how you do it, but finish it. Get rid of that damned house!"

3

John Perkins was angry. "We only got your message last night. We do work. The way it's been going, we'd better work."

He and Cathy sat in Gordon Stewart's office. It was after five-thirty P.M., the building empty and silent.

"And we sometimes go out at night," Cathy said.

"All right," Stewart nodded, "perhaps it's me. My stepson and my wife's first husband are in Fremont, my wife's been upset. I'm sorry, with all the pressure I'm a bit on edge."

"What pressure?" Perkins said.

"Standard, most of it. Don't hurt the community, everyone loses if we don't compromise, we can't win."

"Can we win?" Cathy asked.

"If I didn't think so, I wouldn't advise going on."

"Not even for the principle?" she said.

"The principle is important, Mrs. Perkins, but the interests of my clients come first. If you doubt that—"

"We don't," Perkins said. "Why did you want to see us?"

Stewart swiveled in his chair. "There's one bit of pressure that isn't standard. My stepson came to see me on Monday. He hinted that you two are in this for some other reason than saving your house. The implication was that you're doing something to your advantage that's at least unethical and could ruin our case if it were known."

"That's ridiculous!" Perkins snapped.

"What could we be doing?" Cathy said.

"Who the devil is this stepson?" Perkins said.

"His name's Bill Mackay, he's something of a self-appointed protector of the good, proper, and conservative in country, state, and community. At the moment he works for State Senator Eller, apparently on his campaign for attorney general."

"Well you can tell him we're in this to live in the house we want, where we want, and that's all!"

Stewart studied them both in the silence of the dim office, dusk already settling over the city outside.

"If you did do anything to discredit yourselves, endanger the case, I'd have to resign."

"But people would want to know why!" Cathy said. "It would make us look bad, and that would hurt our case!"

"What could we do that would change any facts?" Perkins said.

Stewart shook his head. "Not the facts, the intent. Our legal system tends to favor the liars because it demands proof of any statement. Without outside evidence or witnesses, the truth and the lie are equal. Credibility, appearance, and in a civil matter like this, intent, become vital. You as the challengers of the norm must be above reproach."

The Perkinses sat silent. Cathy glanced at her husband. The slightly heavy young architect brushed at his short hair.

"All we want is our house," he said.

20

"I hope so," Stewart said. "Real estate is the lifeblood of small cities and semirural towns. The action, the power, in any medium-sized community. People live on it, invest their futures in it. It involves banks, construction companies, builders, unions, lumberyards, everyone. Intentionally or not, you two have attacked the real estate market. Only water rights in Arizona could be more explosive in a community."

"We want our house," Perkins said. "It's our right."

"All we have to do is convince a judge." Stewart smiled, and then, as the Perkinses got up to leave, frowned. "One thing, whatever my stepson is up to, he wouldn't even pretend to want to help me unless he had a reason. I have a strong hunch that Senator Eller's future isn't his only interest in this, so be alert. Bill can be dangerous."

Perkins nodded, and the couple left. Stewart's secretary came in as they went out. ,

"Don't forget Prosecutor Tucker's rally tonight," she said.

Stewart covered his eyes wearily, but he nodded.

"I'll eat downtown, Judy, go over early."

*

The posters and banners proclaimed: TUCKER—The ATTORNEY in Attorney General. The workers, in Tucker sashes, circulated through the ballroom of The Fremont House hotel, or answered questions at small booths set up for each major election issue. The man himself, County Prosecutor Charles Tucker, stood inside the main doors of the ballroom, smiling, shaking hands.

Tucker was a tall man at six-foot-three, thin, and with a youthful face. Now thirty-eight, he was on the way up. Where he wanted to go was to the governorship, and he was trying for the first statewide rung as attorney general. His voice was brisk and firm as he greeted Gordon Stewart.

"In my corner, Gordon?"

"I'm not sure you should let me be," Stewart said.

"The Perkins house? Can you postpone until after election?"

"My clients have suffered enough worry and delay as it is. They want to relax in the house, start living normally again."

"Can they, Gordon? There'll be appeals."

"I have to try, Charley."

"I guess you do."

John Perkins and Cathy watched Stewart and Tucker from across the mammoth room.

"Look at that, John," Cathy said, "like cronies. Real estate is the power, he said it himself."

"And Tucker needs the power to get elected. I know."

"Was that talk of resigning meant to prepare us, John?"

"I hope not," Perkins said, "but what could that stepson of his have been talking about?"

"If the stepson talked about anything."

Perkins was silent. Then he said, "Is there anything this Mackay could know?"

"Not that I know," Cathy said. She looked away.

The crowd grew with the evening. Candidate Tucker moved closer to the podium as the time for speeches approached. Colonel Benjamin Hillock and developer George Spira moved with him.

"It's splitting the town, Charley," Spira said. "Where do individual rights end, and community rights begin?"

"I've got a big investment in my house," Colonel Hillock said. "Will you protect investment, or let any nightmare be built?"

"A community is built on people making compromises for a workable balance," Spira said. "One maverick can ruin that balance if he's allowed to."

22

"Other communities will be watching," Hillock said.

The speeches began and ended, the questions were asked and answered, and Charles Tucker sat alone with his campaign manager. They watched Gordon Stewart leave arguing angrily with Colonel Hillock.

"Charley," the manager said, "if this Perkins thing goes to court you're going to have to take a position."

"What position? Eller can only go one way; he won't get pro-Perkins voters anyway. But I need some votes from all sides and the middle. Whatever I say, I lose."

"You'll lose it all staying silent or neutral. Unless—"

"Damn Perkins, damn Stewart, damn that Mar Vista bunch!"

"If we could keep a lid on it until after election."

"It's ready for trial. How do we stop it?"

"Any damned way we can!"

*

Four miles south of Fremont, Cuyama Beach is a small community of the old rich and the new management aristocracy. Set in the wooded hills and high bluffs of the shoreline above clean, narrow, isolated beaches, it is a mixture of large new ranch houses waiting for hibiscus and trumpet vine to blend them into the rolling countryside, and big old frame houses on their acres of trees behind thick hedges.

The rambling two-story white house on Beacon Road stood behind a high pittosporum hedge on two wooded acres with no lawn. It had not been painted in some years, the brush was thick except directly around the old house, and the flower beds were sparse and scraggly. A large, detached garage had outside stairs going up to an apartment over it. There was light in the downstairs windows of the house.

Barbara Stewart stood in the living room of comfortable

23

old furniture. Pale under her dark tan, she moved stiffly in a gray pantsuit. Bill Mackay lounged on a big, old couch.

"You helping Gordon defend those nuts? Or maybe you're closer to Hansen, eh?"

"What do you want here?"

"Can't a son visit his mama?" Mackay laughed. "You've seen that house? What kind of people could live there? All I can think of is Perkins is out to get attention, make a name with the far-out types who always want to change everything. Build his reputation if it ruins the neighborhood. Gordon say anything like that? About what Perkins is really doing?"

"No. I don't know. I—" She turned away, awkward. "He was a good father to you."

"He did fine. I like how I turned out. The trouble is the wrong kinds fool him too easily. This Perkins and his wife—"

Barbara turned. Sharply. "Gordon's a better person than either of us! He didn't get very much when he got us!"

"No? Haven't you made him happy, Barbara?"

She turned again, walked to the high, old-fashioned front windows with their small, leaded panes. "I don't want you here. You bring nothing but ugliness."

"It'll be my house someday. You've got no one else."

She remained at the window, her back stiff.

"Grace and the kids'll be down. We figured we'd stay here, unless you want to throw us out," Mackay said.

"All right." Her back was still turned to him. "Your family is welcome to any comfort I can give. I don't expect they have an easy life."

"Who said life was supposed to be easy? Fun, exciting, challenging and demanding, maybe, but not easy."

She was silent, watching the night through the windows. Mackay stood up.

24

"Well, I've got business. Grace might be down tomorrow or the next day." He watched his mother's back. "You're sure you can't tell me anything about Gordon and the Perkinses?"

Barbara neither answered nor turned. She went on looking out at the unbroken black of the rural night.

*

Gordon Stewart locked the heavy garage door and crossed through the ragged underbrush beneath the trees in the dark October night. A cool sea wind blew, and the big white house of peeling paint was silent, a single second-floor window showing light. Stewart looked at the neglected house, and then up toward the one lighted window. He went inside.

The dim entry hall was cold. A staircase wound up beyond the archway into the living room. Blue night lights glowed at the foot and top of the stairs. Stewart went past the stairs into the kitchen at the back of the house. He opened the refrigerator, stood there looking in and rubbing at his eyes. He closed the refrigerator. He was suddenly not hungry, too full of beer from the rally, and too tired.

He went up the stairs. A thin line of light came from under Barbara's bedroom door. Stewart could hear her moving behind the door, the clink of ice in a glass.

Stewart put his hand on the doorknob. He stood there for some time, listening to his wife's movements, the sounds of drinking.

He dropped his hand, turned away.

He went down and out of the house and back across the dark grounds under the trees to the garage. He climbed the outside stairs to the small apartment above the garage.

*

Barbara Stewart stood at the small window at the far end of the upstairs hall. A drink in her hand, still dressed in the gray pantsuit, she looked down at the light in the garage apartment.

The light went out.

Barbara remained at the window, drinking and listening to the silence of the big old house.

When the drink was empty, she turned and went down the stairs.

*

Much later the telephone began to ring in the house. It rang unanswered for a long time.

Across Beacon Road a figure stood in the shadows of the trees and listened to the telephone ring.

Somewhere near three A.M. the figure watched a car turn into the grounds of the big white house. The figure crossed the road and moved closer to the house. The car had stopped in front of the closed garage.

Forty-five minutes later the car came out of the driveway and turned north toward Fremont.

The figure reappeared, returned to the shadows of the trees across the dark night road from the house.

Toward dawn another car turned into the grounds and stopped in front of the house. Some fifteen minutes later it left again.

*

County Prosecutor Charles Tucker stood alone in the small apartment over the garage of the white house on Beacon Road. He looked at the bed in the morning light. He looked at his watch.

He stood there chewing on his lips for some time.

Then he went to the telephone.

4

County Prosecutor's Investigator Lee Beckett drove out of San Vicente, the county seat of Buena Costa County, in the clear October morning. A heavy-shouldered man in his fifties, as thick as he was wide, Beckett seemed shorter than his six feet. His gray hair was cropped short and his blue eyes were sunk in wind creases. He drove fast on Highway 101 north.

Once a New York City detective captain, Beckett had come west to Buena Costa County to find a new life when an addict's bomb put him in the hospital, killed one son, and crippled his wife. His wife had died within a year, and Beckett had joined the Sheriff's Department. That lasted only until John Hoag was elected sheriff. Unable to work with Hoag, he retired to operate the nursery he had started as a hobby. Coaxed back to work by Prosecutor Charles Tucker himself, he was now Tucker's top investigator, and his eyes were troubled as he drove.

The freeway goes west beyond San Vicente, the sea blue to the south bordered by clean public county beaches and the lush vegetation of the coastal strip. It turns north through narrow Los Cruces Pass where the brown Santa Ysolde Mountains come to the sea, and twelve miles beyond the pass Highway 1 leads to Fremont.

The third largest city in Buena Costa County, Fremont was until very recently an industrial town of thirty thousand with canneries, fertilizer factories, oil refineries and petrochemical plants. A grimy city without mountains or natural beauty except the wide ocean outside its polluted harbor. It was still most of that, but Beckett was aware of the changes of the last year.

In a time of soaring real estate prices brought on by a growing population and moratoriums on building, those of more modest and fixed incomes, and the young just starting out, are pushed into the less desirable areas such as Fremont. Still a town of treeless streets, cheap tract houses, and industrial slums, its population had grown to nearly forty thousand, the harbor had been cleaned up, and the smoke almost eliminated by a city council that saw profit in the air. Expensive developments were going up all around the periphery, moving inexorably down toward the homes of the town leaders in Cuyama Beach.

Beckett drove more slowly through the small, elegant village of Cuyama Beach with its beach clubs, fenced beaches, and plush boat marina. He followed the winding rural roads past the new ranch houses, the Spanish-style villas on the terraced hills, and the big old houses in the woods. The Stewart house on Beacon Road was one of the old houses, big and white. Beckett parked in front of the closed garage.

"Here, Lee!" Charles Tucker stood at the top of the flight of outside stairs on the garage.

Inside the small, neat, fully furnished apartment Beckett looked at the man in the bed. Under the covers, Gordon Stewart could have been asleep. But his open eyes stared at

28

nothing, his mouth gaped, and his sleep was permanent.

"Not a mark on him," Tucker said. "I looked."

Beckett sniffed. "The room smells like a garage."

"Monoxide? An accident? Suicide?"

"Any note?"

"Not that I can see."

"You called the Fremont Sheriff's Station?"

"Not yet."

Beckett watched the prosecutor in silence.

"They'd want to know why I was here. When I got here."

"Why are you here, Charley?"

"You've heard about the damned cube house mess?"

"I heard something."

"It's a political bombshell. I lose votes no matter which side I favor, or if I stay neutral. I came to try to talk Stewart into postponing going to court, hold it under wraps, until after the election. There wasn't much chance, but I had to try." Tucker's hands shaped the air of the room as if he were summing up for a jury. "I got here about eight o'clock. There was no answer at the house. I heard music coming from this apartment. I found him. The clock-radio was blaring as if he'd set it to wake him at eight. I shut it off, called you."

Beckett looked toward the dead man. "I'd say he died before eight, probably an accident. What's the problem? Why call me instead of the substation or Hoag himself?"

"The problem is why was I visiting him at eight in the morning at his house. It's got political 'deal' written all over it! The county prosecutor and candidate for attorney general trying to influence a civil case! If Hoag knows I was here he'll make sure everyone in the county knows. He's behind Eller."

"So?"

Tucker studied his hands. "Is there any way you can keep me out of it?"

Beckett was silent. "I told you politics would get you in trouble, Charley."

"I'll be a good attorney general, Lee. Someday I'll be a good governor, too."

"Yeh," Beckett said, "if you're still the same man by the time you become governor."

"Can you find a reason to say you found him?"

Beckett didn't answer. While Tucker watched him, he began to move slowly around the whole apartment. He examined the single door. It had an old-fashioned key lock that did not seem to have been locked in some time. A bottle of pills stood on the night table. Nembutal, the bottle over half full. Beckett leaned close to the dead man's gaping mouth.

"Smells a little like beer."

"He drank beer at my rally."

Beckett bent and picked something from the floor near the bed. It was a small green pin-on button with gold lettering.

"Mar Vista Civic Association. Why would he have this?"

"I don't know, Lee. Maybe he picked it up on some visit to their office, but I don't see why he would."

Beckett slipped the button into his pocket, stood at the dresser looking at the contents of Stewart's pockets laid out there. There was a wallet with credit cards, bills and loose change, a small notebook, and a cigarette lighter.

"Let's look in the garage," Beckett said.

They went down. The heavy garage door was locked. They circled the garage. There were two windows and a side door. The door was unlocked. Inside, they found a compact Chevrolet Nova and a big Cadillac Fleetwood. Beckett felt both hoods. There was a strong odor of exhaust in the garage. Beckett raised both hoods, felt each radiator and hose.

"The Caddy's still a little warm."

He opened the driver's door of the Cadillac. Then he went to the rear of the big car. A small gravity furnace stood in a corner of the garage close behind the Cadillac.

"His keys are still in the Caddy. I figured they would be when they weren't with his other stuff. I guess he just left the motor running, Charley. An accident. I can tell Hoag I came to see him, keep you out of it."

"Lee," Tucker said. "Stewart wasn't driving the Caddy last night. He had the Nova, I saw him. His wife used the Caddy for her real estate work. More comfortable, you know?"

Beckett was silent. "It could be suicide, but why bother to change cars? Then, if he'd wanted to kill himself, he had enough pills to do it a lot simpler and easier."

"Murder, Lee?"

"I don't know, but the Caddy exhaust is right on top of that furnace duct up to the apartment. You better call Hoag yourself, Charley. No lies now."

Tucker looked at the Cadillac, and at the furnace duct that went up into the apartment above.

"Maybe I didn't really want to be governor anyway."

*

It was just before seven-thirty A.M. when Maxwell Bowman drove his Mercedes sedan into his driveway. He got out and stood in the gray dawn staring at the windowless wall of the Perkins house. His whole body was tense, and he ran his hands through his white hair. His lips moved as if muttering some incantation or prayer that would make the horrible house vanish.

As he turned to go into his own house, he stopped. He had heard movement in the Perkins house. He listened.

Someone was up in the cube house. Bowman looked at his watch, stared again at the hated house, but there were no windows in the long blank wall to reveal who was up. He went into his house.

"Maxwell? Is that you? Where have you been?"

Bowman went into the bedroom.

"Stewart's dead," he said.

"Stewart?" Estelle Bowman blinked.

"The lawyer for the Perkinses."

"Oh? He wasn't very old, was he? It must have been sudden, I . . . But look at the time! I had no idea it was almost eight. I must get my ranunculus planted, I'm late already."

Bowman watched her get out of bed and pad into the bathroom babbling on about the ranunculus.

*

A half-heard noise awakened John Perkins. His head ached from drinking too much at the Tucker rally and later with Cathy talking about the house past midnight. He rarely drank that much, and felt guilty as he lay in bed. Depressed and vulnerable. Was the house becoming too much in their lives?

He turned to Cathy. She wasn't there. Her side of the bed untouched, not slept in. Perkins got up.

Fully dressed, Cathy sat at the kitchen table with a glass of milk. The clock read seven-thirty. She went to work at nine.

"You're up early," Perkins said.

"Office crisis. How do you feel?"

"Like a man who drank too much. No breakfast?"

"I'm late already."

"Why didn't you mention this crisis last night?"

She smiled. "I did."

"I was that bad? Where did you sleep?"

32

"In the guest room. You were snoring like a bear." She finished her milk, stood up. "I'd better go."

"Cath? You want to give up? Sell for what we can get?"

Her eyes were black in her round face. "No! We won't give up. Not now. We'll go all the way."

She left without kissing him. He stood looking at the door until he heard her drive away. He went into the guest room. Both twin beds were made.

In the bedroom he undressed for his shower. She was a neat woman. Even without time for breakfast she would have made her bed. He was sure of that.

*

Behind the office of Hansen Realty in the stucco bungalow on the Fremont side street were the living room, bedroom, bathroom and kitchen Phil Hansen kept for his private use.

Hansen sat in the small living room and listened to the clock out in the office chime eight o'clock. In his shirtsleeves, the big real estate man rubbed at the beard stubble on his handsome face and watched the sleeping Barbara Stewart through the open bedroom door. With her blond hair spread around her thin face on the pillow she always seemed younger.

Hansen stretched, took his suit coat out from under her clothes piled on a chair, and went to shave.

*

Mrs. Patricia Hillock lit another cigarette and looked out the front window of her two-story colonial house in Mar Vista.

"Busy neighbors this morning. Max Bowman's been out already, and the Perkins woman just drove off in a hurry."

The man on the couch stood up. "I can't wait for Ben any longer, Pat. Tell him what's happening down at the camp, okay?"

He was a short, nervous man in an Army uniform with the silver bars of a captain. He moved toward the door.

"He's only around Dresden, Casey," Pat Hillock said, "but when he's hunting you never know when he'll get back."

"That why you were still up when I got here?"

"Just couldn't sleep," she said. "Thanks for coming, Casey."

"Yeh," the captain said. "I expect it'll blow over."

"Let's hope so," Patricia Hillock said.

*

George Spira went to work very early that morning. When his office staff began to arrive, they found Spira already at his desk.

*

Sheriff John Hoag examined the garage. His men worked over the Cadillac, spread across the grounds, swarmed in the apartment above, and moved into the main house. Tucker and Beckett were with him. Hoag went up to the apartment. The assistant coroner was busy with the body. Hoag examined the bed table, the bureau, and the floor register from the furnace below.

"Okay," he said, "what were you doing here, Charley?"

"Maybe we should discuss the case a little before you start interrogating suspects," Beckett said.

Hoag turned on the big county investigator. A stocky man in his fifties, Hoag had a smooth, bland face that revealed nothing and offended no one. He wore an ordinary blue business suit, decked out with a white stetson, string tie, and western boots. The sheriff nodded.

"I'll listen. Tell me about the case."

Beckett watched Hoag's men work. "Stewart left Charley's rally around eleven, came home probably tired but full of beer and keyed up too. Maybe something was on his

34

mind, so he took the Nembutal to be sure he'd sleep. The combination—beer, pills, overtired—made him sleep heavily. The exhaust fumes must have come up through that duct like a pipeline, and he was asleep too deep to hear the engine or smell the fumes."

Beckett looked toward the bed. "He couldn't have left the Caddy running by accident, he wasn't driving it. It could be suicide, but why not sit in the car, or use the pills he had? Someone else could have left the car running by accident. Or someone could have taken his keys, used the Caddy to kill him."

The assistant coroner walked up. "It looks like straight monoxide, no wounds. I'll do the autopsy, but say he died between two and four A.M. I don't think he ever woke up or knew what happened. Not a bad way to go."

A fingerprint man reported, "Prints all over the car and the apartment, but they look like him and the family. We've got a couple from the doorknob that could be different."

"Check them out," Hoag said.

"No keys in the apartment," a deputy summed up, "no sign of strangers, nothing not his except maybe that button Beckett found. No one home in the house. Beds weren't slept in, but someone had a drink. Glass and bottle in the kitchen. We've put out a call to find the wife."

"Keep looking around," Hoag said. He faced Tucker. "So we've talked about it, Charley. Now what were you doing here?"

"I came to try to talk Stewart into postponing the Perkins trial," Tucker said.

"Did you?"

"I got here around eight! You heard when he died."

"Anyone see you get here around eight A.M.?"

"Not that I know."

Beckett said, "When do we start getting serious, Hoag?"

"You don't think I'm serious, Beckett?" Hoag said. "The cube house thing is a political bombshell, and calling you instead of us sounds a lot like he had cover-up in mind."

"Then you'd better read me my rights," Tucker said.

"And I better get to work finding out what really happened here," Beckett said.

Hoag's bland face darkened, but he said nothing as Beckett walked out and down the outside stairs.

5

In the warming morning Beckett slowly circled the garage in expanding circles. He found nothing until he came across the flattened area of tall grass. It was about six feet long and four feet wide, ragged and irregular, with most of the weeds and grass crushed flat, but some only bent and broken. It was fifteen feet from the side door of the garage.

As if something had been dumped in the high grass. Or as if someone had been lying hidden there.

Beckett crossed through the underbrush under the trees to the big white house. He inspected the main rooms, saw nothing unusual. In the kitchen he found the bottle of Scotch and the single glass. The glass was empty. Upstairs he went through the master bedroom. The king-sized bed had not been slept in; he found nothing that seemed to be evidence, but there was something definitely unusual. It was the master bedroom of a husband and wife, but there seemed to be nothing in the room that belonged to a husband.

He found three more bedrooms on the second floor. All were furnished, the beds were made and ready, but there was nothing in any of the drawers or closets, and nothing on any of the surfaces. Empty, unused rooms.

Beckett left the house. Under the trees he searched the grounds. A trail of faint marks that could have been footprints led to a narrow gap in the high hedge that bordered Beacon Road. Across the rural road there was a thick grove of trees. Something glinted among the trees.

Beckett crossed the road and picked up a small brass disk with a hole at the top and the number "12" stamped on it. The disk was worn and battered as if from long handling, and the ground in the grove of trees showed that someone had been there recently, pacing back and forth. Beckett returned to the garage.

Charley Tucker had gone, and Sheriff Hoag was talking to a large group of newsmen.

". . . there'll be no special treatment of anyone as long as I'm sheriff in this county, but I'm certain that Prosecutor Tucker has a complete explanation for his presence here," Hoag said, serious and solemn. "Everyone connected to the possible homicide will be investigated—impartially. I'm sure Tucker will give you his own statement later, and after the autopsy we'll know more. Prosecutor Tucker will be exonerated."

The newsmen hurried to their cars. Beckett sat on the bed. The body had been removed.

"I can see the headline," Beckett said. " 'Sheriff denies county prosecutor is murderer!' But what was the candidate for state attorney general doing at such an early hour in the house of the lawyer in the controversial cube house case? You back Senator Eller, right?"

Hoag sat down. "I just gave them the facts."

"Yeh," Beckett said. "Okay, you've had your fun. Now what have you got to go on? Assuming it is murder, and pretending maybe Tucker didn't kill him."

38

Hoag grinned, then shrugged. "Nothing much yet. That Mar Vista button. The fingerprints on the doorknob."

"What about the button? You think the cube house mess is the motive?"

"Stands to reason; feelings are running pretty high over it," Hoag said, expressionless. "On all sides."

"One of the Mar Vista people? Real estate interests?"

"Maybe, but Stewart could have picked up that button himself; he must have gone to the Mar Vista Association office on the case. And if someone against the cube house wanted to get rid of it so much he'd resort to murder, why not kill the Perkinses, end it for good?"

"Too obvious? The motive too certain? By killing Stewart the Perkinses might be scared enough to give up, it'll cause a big delay at least, and the motive would be less certain with more possible suspects?"

Hoag was unconvinced. "Damned thin. How about the Perkins people themselves, one of their backers?"

"Why the hell would they kill their own lawyer?"

"A lot of people don't think they're so clean and pure in all of it, are out for some advantage, have an angle. Could be that Stewart found out what it was, was going to blow the whistle."

"I don't know," Beckett said. "It looks to me like the cube house is a pretty weak motive all around, not really logical. What about some other case he was on, or something personal?"

"We'll look into everything," Hoag said.

"You've sent those doorknob prints to Sacramento, the FBI?"

"No, they were identified as soon as the lab got them. We ran the family through first, they turned out to be the son. The wife's son, Stewart's stepson, Bill Mackay. He lives up in Sacramento, but he's in town now."

"What's he doing in town?"

"Working on Senator Eller's campaign." Hoag's voice was smooth and bland. "He could have left those prints any time. It's his home, you know?"

"He could have," Beckett said. "You're going to find him and the wife?"

"We'll find them." Hoag watched Beckett. "You know, Tucker did want the cube house trial postponed. Now it will be."

"But you'll investigate other motives anyway, right?"

"Of course." Hoag smiled. "Only it'll take some time."

Beckett stood up and walked out. Outside, he took the brass disk from his pocket and studied it for a time. He put it back into his pocket, and walked on to his car.

*

Phil Hansen was at his desk in his bungalow office. Bill Mackay sat down in the client chair.

"The early bird makes the sale," Mackay said. "Been in long?"

"You looking for a house? Going to move back?"

"If I do, I've got a house. The ancestral manse. Is she here?"

Hansen sat back. "I don't think that's any of—"

"Gordon's dead."

"Dead? Stewart? How? What do you mean?"

"Dead means dead."

"No, I mean, what happened? How do you know?"

They both heard the door open. Barbara Stewart stood in the doorway between the office and the private rooms. Her blond hair loose and uncombed on her shoulders, she wore a man's red terry cloth robe too big for her.

"You look cosy, Mother," Bill Mackay said.

"Gordon?" Her voice was ragged, and her eyes moved randomly.

Mackay nodded. He watched her closely. She came into the sunny office holding the robe tightly around her in the chill of the October morning. She sat down, hunched.

"No, Gordon was never sick. You're wrong, William."

"In the apartment over the garage," Mackay said. "And he wasn't sick, not physically anyway."

Hansen said, "The garage?"

"Not Gordon," Barbara said. Her head moved back and forth as if searching for something.

"You've both been here all night?" Mackay asked.

Barbara looked down at the chair she sat in, at the office. Uncertain, she seemed surprised to find herself there.

"All night?" she said. She reddened. "I don't think—"

"Yes," Hansen said, nodded. "We can't hide it now, Barb. We were here all night, we're in love, we—"

"I don't give a damn what you two do; Barbara's a big girl, but it could be damned important. Do you have your car keys, Barbara?"

Her voice was distant. "His heart, was that it? All the stress? I never gave him a very good life, did I?"

"I think he died of monoxide poisoning," Mackay said. "There were keys in the Cadillac. Do you have yours?"

"She has them," Hansen said. "As a matter of fact, I have them. I unlocked the door when we got here last night."

"In your car?"

"I picked her up late, we had a few drinks, came here."

"Phil?" Barbara said.

"They'll find out now, Barb. Everyone. We better tell about last night. About all the nights." Hansen shifted uneasily in the desk chair. "You think he left the car running?"

"Maybe," Mackay said, "maybe not. He wasn't driving the Caddy last night. He'd emptied his pockets up on his bureau. He'd taken some pills, was up late drinking. He must have been heavy asleep, never woke up. Maybe someone took his keys."

"Took?" Hansen said. "You mean—murder?"

Mackay scowled. "I've got a hunch there's more to this cube house thing than we know. Those Perkinses are up to something, some angle. I told Gordon about it, maybe he found out more, was going to quit the case. Or maybe the Perkinses were just afraid he would find out and leave them cold."

"That could have hurt their case, made them look bad. Especially if some scheme came out."

"Especially."

"What do the police say?"

"I wouldn't know," Mackay said. "I didn't report it. I wanted to talk to Barbara first. But the way I see it, there's accident or murder. Nothing else."

Hansen nodded. "I can't think of anything else. He left the car running, or someone killed him. Right, Barbara?"

Her darkly tanned face was drawn, detached. "Poor Gordon. He should have had a better life."

"Shouldn't everyone," Mackay said. He got up. "I don't think he left the Caddy running, and that's a big can of worms. It's going to be trouble for those Perkinses one way or another, so I think we should all keep cool and quiet. Right?"

Hansen nodded, thoughtful. "What time did you say you found him this morning? How'd you happen to be there?"

"About six-thirty. My family's coming down, I wanted to be sure everything was set for them."

"At six-thirty A.M.?"

"I'm an early bird too," Mackay said.

Hansen said nothing. Barbara Stewart sat hunched in the ill-fitting man's robe as if she wasn't even there.

*

Sheriff John Hoag drove into the dusty yard of Spira Construction Company. He found George Spira behind his desk in the second floor office that looked out over the whole yard and the ranks of heavy equipment.

"Gordon Stewart's dead. It looks like murder." Hoag told the stocky developer all that had happened. He rubbed his hands. "Charley Tucker's got big trouble."

"Did he do it?" Spira said.

"Hell, I doubt it, but we can make nice hay out of it. You better make sure all your Mar Vista people have alibis."

"You mean find out *if* they have alibis, don't you? You mean investigate them?" Spira said.

Hoag cooled. "Did I say different?"

"I thought I heard different," Spira said. "I thought I heard politics. Tucker did something, or he didn't. Period."

"I thought you were a Republican. Against Tucker and that cube house."

"I'm a Republican, and the Mar Vista Association is against the cube house. I'm not much for radical reactionaries like Senator Eller, the cube house doesn't bother me that much personally, and I haven't decided about Tucker yet."

"He's one of those big-government, big-handout liberals!"

"What do you think Jesse Eller's big business friends live on, Hoag? Subsidies, government contracts, tax breaks and tax protection!" Spira said, scornful. He glanced out his window at the construction yard. "You're sure Stewart was murdered?"

"Pretty sure," Hoag said. "Where were you last night?"

"Me?" Spira continued to look out his window. "Home. I went straight home after Tucker's rally. Came to work early."

"You live alone, right?"

43

"You think I killed him?"

"You've got a lot of money invested in Mar Vista."

"It's a motive," Spira said.

"Yes it is," Hoag said.

George Spira stared out his window for some time after Hoag had gone. Then he turned to the telephone.

"Bowman? We've got to talk. Get Colonel Hillock."

*

Lee Beckett stood in Gordon Stewart's outer office. The girl at the desk was young. She looked up. A large girl with short black hair.

"I'm sorry, the counselor isn't here."

"I know," Beckett said. "Miss—?"

"Muldahr, Judy Muldahr. He should be here soon, he didn't say he'd be late. You can wait, or leave your name."

"Stewart won't be in, Miss Muldahr." He told her. "I'm sorry."

She sat there. Her hand went up to her mouth. She began to chew on her thumb.

"Do you know where his wife is? Or her son? Mackay?"

"No." She went on biting her thumb, not moving.

"Can I get you something? Some water?"

"No." She was young, having trouble with death. "He was right here. Just last night. He ate in town." She smiled, and stopped. "It's true? Really? I mean, he's really—?"

"It's true," Beckett said. "Can you think of anyone who'd want to kill him, Miss Muldahr? Any difficult cases?"

She shook her head.

"Angry clients, recent bad cases? Anyone he was uneasy about, had doubts about?"

She took a long breath. "The only real trial he had just now is the Perkins house case. No criminal cases. A couple of estate probates, his corporation work. Not even a divorce."

44

"I'd better look at his files."

She chewed a fingernail. "I . . . I mean they're confidential. Without a court order or something I don't think I—"

"All right," Beckett said. He took out the small brass disk he'd found on Beacon Road. "Have you ever seen this before?"

She shook her head. "No."

"Did he have any personal troubles you know about?"

"No. I mean, he was worried about his wife, she seemed kind of funny when she was here last, but I don't know why. And he had an argument with Mr. Spira over something about the Perkins case. But that's all."

"The Mar Vista developer?"

She nodded. "He was very angry about the Perkinses just last night. He said they were doing something unethical, and maybe he was going to quit the case."

"You heard him say he might quit the case?"

"Well, I think that's what he said."

"You don't know what he'd learned about the Perkinses?"

"No."

*

Judy Muldahr still sat at the desk when the door to the private office opened behind her.

"You did that just fine," Bill Mackay said.

She didn't turn. "I don't like to lie, Bill."

"Sometimes you lie to protect the truth." Mackay came and sat on the edge of the desk. "But you weren't lying. The Perkinses are up to some scheme, Gordon did know about it. I know it, I just didn't want the cops to know I knew yet."

"Why didn't you want his files examined?"

"The liberals love court orders, they should practice what they preach."

"Why didn't he know you found Mr. Stewart?"

45

"Because I didn't tell anyone. I had some things to do first. Hey, Judy, I'm back!"

He smiled, leaned down and kissed her. After a moment her arms went around his neck and she clung tightly.

"Your place later," Mackay said. "I'll call."

She nodded. He kissed her lightly again, stood up.

"You never did like Mr. Stewart, did you, Bill?"

"No, I never liked him."

"Your mother has that money."

Mackay smiled. "Be ready later, I feel like a bull."

6

The Mar Vista Civic Association office was on the second floor of a shopping center building where all the offices opened onto an outside balcony. Beckett found the door locked. A typed card instructed visitors to contact George Spira or Maxwell Bowman and gave their addresses.

Beckett stopped his car at the side of the road where the cube house stood above on a knoll. It was like no house he had ever seen. Designed to fit the narrow lot when not much else would have, probably efficient and comfortable inside, and when the rough siding had weathered and the landscaping filled in, it wouldn't be all that visible or bizarre. Beckett found it imaginative, and he shook his head over what people would fight about as he drove off on the access road and turned into the driveway of Maxwell Bowman's ranch house.

A stout, gray-haired woman in baggy slacks, a long flowered smock, and broad-brimmed straw hat opened the door.

"Mrs. Bowman? May I speak to your husband?"

"Oh, yes, come in. Maxwell! Someone to see you. He

was just about to go out, you're lucky to have caught him. I'm getting in my ranunculus, you'll excuse my appearance. It's very late already. I'm afraid, Mr.—?''

She chattered nonstop while she led Beckett into a large, bright living room stuffed with heavy furniture and floral slip covers on beige wall-to-wall carpet.

"Beckett," he said.

"Of Beckett Nursery in San Vicente? And here I am telling you about ranunculus! I always have good luck with mine, or I always did. This year . . . Oh, there you are, Maxwell."

The small, white-haired man came into the living room with the quick movements of a terrier. Brisk and impatient in shirt, tie, gray slacks and a blue blazer, he was obviously anxious to be going somewhere. He stopped short when he saw Beckett, his face closed and suspicious.

"Lee Beckett, Mr. Bowman, County Prosecutor's Office. I'd like to ask you some questions."

"About what?"

"I'm afraid that Gordon Stewart, the lawyer for your cube house opponents, was killed last night."

"Oh, Maxwell knows about poor Mr. Stewart. So tragic, such a young man. Maxwell told me about it this morning."

"Estelle," Bowman said.

"What time this morning?" Beckett said.

"About seven-thirty, I'd say. I overslept again, Maxwell had been out in the car already." Estelle Bowman frowned. "I've been oversleeping a lot lately, I . . . Well, never mind. It was about seven-thirty, wasn't it, Maxwell?"

"About," Maxwell Bowman said.

"Well," Estelle said, "I must to work. I'll visit your nursery, Mr. Beckett. I do hope my ranunculus aren't too late."

She smiled to both of them, and hurried out toward the rear of the house. Bowman stared after her.

48

"It's all hit her so hard she won't recognize it exists," Bowman said. "Everything is normal."

"You were out in your car, came home at seven-thirty and knew Stewart was dead. He wasn't discovered until past eight."

Bowman continued to stare toward where his wife had gone.

"I had a call from Bill Mackay. I met him at his motel. He told me."

"Stewart's stepson?"

"Yes."

"He knew you'd be interested?"

Bowman walked around. "I knew Mackay before he went up to Sacramento; we think alike, so I got him to do some work for me. It's no secret I'm interested in anything that will get rid of that damned house out there."

"Mackay's helping you to get rid of it?"

"I hope so, yes."

"Any way he can?"

Bowman stopped short. "I resent that, Beckett."

"Mackay apparently knew Stewart was dead before anyone else. He must have been at the house. When?"

"It's his home! The man was his stepfather!"

"Yeh," Beckett said. "Where were you before Mackay called you?"

"Here."

"Alone?"

"With my wife and in bed. I didn't kill him, why would I?"

Beckett looked out Bowman's front window at the towering blank wall of the cube house. "I can think of some reasons. You hate that house. Perhaps Stewart was persuading other Mar Vista people to compromise. Perhaps you knew you'd lose in court."

"We won't lose," Bowman said. "If you're looking for

suspects, when I got home this morning someone was already up in the Perkinses house. They never get up that early. I've never seen either of them leave before eight-thirty, and today the wife drove off long before eight!''

"Why would they want to kill Stewart?''

"Who knows what people like that might do!''

Bowman glared out his window at the cube house.

*

Naked, drying himself after his shower, Colonel Benjamin Hillock stood up from his chair to look out the bedroom window. His body was lean and muscled, the stomach still flat. With his bald head and gray mustache, it gave the illusion of two different men in the same space. His wife watched his body.

"There's a man coming out of Max Bowman's house and going over to the Perkinses,'' Hillock said. "I know him, yeh. Lee Beckett, an investigator for Prosecutor Tucker's office.''

"Didn't Spira say Tucker was somehow mixed up in Stewart's murder?'' Patricia Hillock said. "Maybe Beckett's after other suspects. Bowman and Cathy Perkins were both out early this morning.''

Hillock finished drying himself. "You say Casey thinks it'll all blow over down at the base? No inquiry?''

"That's what he said, but Casey's not the brightest captain the Army ever had. You'd better go down and check yourself.''

"Casey was my best exec officer,'' Hillock said. "You never thought any army man was too bright, did you? Why the hell did you marry a soldier?''

"I was young.''

Hillock dressed. "Damn! This cube house screw-up is getting out of hand. Our house won't be worth sixty percent of what we hoped soon. Who the hell could have killed Stewart?''

"You're sure you were out hunting pigs?''

"Cute," Hillock said. He tied his tie. "I don't think you better suggest that idea to anyone else.''

"Not that I'd blame you. Stewart was the best chance they had to keep that circus house parked in our lap.''

In a silence, Hillock finished dressing. He studied his appearance in the mirror. He didn't seem to like himself much in the gray business suit.

"Didn't you say you were still up when Casey came this morning?'' he said. "Five A.M.?''

"Too many worries to sleep," Patricia Hillock said. "You really had better go down to the old base and talk to Casey. The others too. A lot of them must still be our friends. Casey said the new colonel isn't so popular.''

"So now you're worried about it all?''

"You're not worried?''

"I was worried before we began. It was your idea.''

"You're damned right it was! You owed me for all those years of Army posts. The Army owed me!''

"All right," Hillock said. "First I'll see what Spira wants, then I'll go down there. It'll work out.''

"It better," Pat Hillock said.

*

No one was home at the cube house. Beckett stopped at a gas station to call Judy Muldahr in Gordon Stewart's office and find out where Cathy Perkins worked.

On the highway toward San Vicente, the Ocean Sciences, Inc., building was a small, one-story Spanish style with the parking lot at the side. The editorial department was at the rear. Cathy Perkins was working at her desk.

"Mrs. Perkins?''

The woman was small, with a round, girlish face and dark

51

brown eyes. She smiled, but there were shadows around her eyes.

"Yes."

"Lee Beckett, Mrs. Perkins, from the County Prosecutor's Office. Has the sheriff been in touch with you yet?"

"The sheriff?" She stopped smiling. "No. Has something happened? To John? Is he—?"

"Gordon Stewart, your lawyer, was killed last night."

She stared up at Beckett. A deep breath of relief, and then the relief vanished as fast as her smile had. Alarm in her shadowed eyes.

"Mr. Stewart? Killed? You mean—?"

"We're not certain, but it looks like murder, yes."

"But . . . why? Who? I mean—" Her deep breath was slow this time. "You think it was something to do with our case?"

"It's possible, Mrs. Perkins. Feelings are running high about your house," Beckett said. "You left your house earlier than usual this morning."

"Me? Yes, I had to come in to work early."

"You mind if I check that with your boss?"

They faced each other in a silence. Through the small editorial room other people talked, laughed. A few of her co-workers glanced curiously toward where Beckett stood over her.

"I didn't come in early. I had some private business."

"You mind telling me what?"

"Yes, I mind! Do you think I killed Mr. Stewart?"

"Not if you didn't leave your house before seven-thirty."

"I didn't!"

Beckett said, "I've been told that Stewart had learned that you and your husband were doing something unethical, and that he was going to quit your case."

52

"It's a lie! Who told you that?"

"His secretary."

"Well she's wrong! Mr. Stewart was sure we'd win! If anyone killed him it was our enemies! They hate our house!"

She glared up at Beckett.

*

Maxwell Bowman shifted in the chair in George Spira's office. Colonel Benjamin Hillock stood in his gray suit looking out the window at the busy construction yard below.

"Either of you kill him?" George Spira said.

Hillock didn't bother to turn around. He just laughed.

"Did you?" Bowman said. "What kind of question is that, Spira?"

"No, I didn't, and it's a straight question. There could be a reasonable explanation, and we could agree on what to do from here on. But if there isn't, we all have the same motive, so we better get our facts straight. Where were we all last night? I was home alone, I have no alibi."

"I was hunting over beyond Dresden," Colonel Hillock said. "Alone, all night, I didn't shoot any pigs."

"Dresden isn't thirty miles away."

"I didn't shoot any men either."

Bowman said, "Stewart wasn't shot. Monoxide from a car."

"Hoag talked to you too?" Spira said.

"Some county investigator named Beckett," Bowman said. "But I already knew about Stewart anyway."

At the window, Hillock turned to look at Bowman. Spira stabbed his letter opener into his memo pad. Bowman shifted again in his chair.

"I had a call this morning from Bill Mackay, Stewart's stepson. About six-thirty, he wanted to see me. I went to his motel. He told me he'd found Stewart dead in an apartment over his garage.''

"Why did this Mackay call you?" Hillock said. "Who is he anyway?"

"He's doing some work for me," Bowman said.

"And I'll tell you who he is," Spira said. "He's a self-proclaimed right-wing vigilante who doesn't give a damn what methods he uses to 'protect' the country from radicals! He and Stewart couldn't stand each other after Mackay grew up. He got in so much hot water here he went up to Sacramento to work for Jesse Eller as a hatchet man! What did you hire him to do, Bowman?"

"To help us get rid of that damned house!"

"How? Or don't you care?" Spira said angrily. "When some of Mackay's neighbors had a beef a few years ago, came to talk to him, he met them with a pair of guns in his belt! He once jumped out of a second-story window to scare some noisy teenagers. He even slapped one kid around!"

"He thinks right," Bowman said. "He'll do something, not just talk or trust some damned liberal court!"

Hillock said, "Maybe he already has."

7

The campus of Fremont State University is north of the city on flat land surrounded by small industrial plants and a large refinery. It was past noon when Beckett met John Perkins as he came out of a class.

"Lee Beckett, County Prosecutor's Office, Mr. Perkins. You've heard about Gordon Stewart?"

"Yes," John Perkins said. The heavyish young architect glanced around at all the passing students. "I only share an office out here. We can talk over at the athletic field."

They sat in the wooden stands above the empty playing field and deserted track.

"Why was Stewart going to drop your case?" Beckett said.

"He wasn't going to drop us," Perkins said. He looked out across the stadium. "But perhaps someone wanted him to. He told us just last night that his stepson had accused us of having a scheme to use the house for some special benefit. Neither my wife nor I had, or have, any idea what he was talking about, and Stewart wasn't going to quit."

A scrawny youth had begun to run steadily around the

oval track. Some girls in blue jeans, and their short-haired blond young men, sat out on the field smoking and drinking beer.

"You know your wife didn't go to her office early this morning? She had some private business?"

The girls on the grass laughed at the solitary runner.

"We have no secrets," Perkins said.

"You know what the business was?"

"Of course, but it's a personal matter."

"Too personal to tell about?"

Perkins nodded.

"Where were you last night and this morning?"

"At home in bed. I drank too much at Tucker's rally, and later. It seems I slept it off."

"Your wife got up first?"

"She was up when I awoke."

"Up? Dressed. You didn't see her get up, or know when?"

Perkins watched the lone runner circling the track.

"You must have been sleeping heavily," Beckett said.

Perkins said, "Isn't it possible he wasn't killed because of our house at all? Or over some aspect of the whole affair that only incidentally involves our case? For example, last night Stewart warned us that his stepson was a dangerous man who probably had some other reason for mixing in the case than helping Senator Eller get elected."

"Yes," Beckett said, "it's possible."

*

Barbara Stewart lay on the bed in Phil Hansen's private rooms behind the bungalow office. She watched the early afternoon sunlight through the open windows. Hansen smoked in the bedroom doorway.

"Don't you think you'd better go home?" Hansen said. "The cops have to be looking for you."

"I killed him, Phil, didn't I?"

"Don't be stupid!"

"Me! My fault!"

Hansen smoked, studied her face turned up now to the ceiling of the sunny room.

"All right, you killed him. Maybe we both did. But he's dead, what can you do for him now? How bad do you want it to look? To the cops? In the newspapers?"

"Look? Can it look worse?"

"A lot, Barb. Right now it's murder or an accident. If they start thinking about suicide, the injured husband, it'll be splashed all over everything, the full spotlight. I don't need that, neither do you."

"No, we wouldn't want that, would we?"

Hansen stubbed out his cigarette in an ashtray. He ground it out viciously.

"You going to fall apart on me?"

"Haven't I already? Now and always? Useless."

Hansen went and sat on the edge of the bed beside her. She didn't look at him. He took her hand.

"Barb, listen. We can really go places now. You and me. We can—"

Outside in the office the outer door opened and closed with a slam. Heavy feet strode. "Hansen!" It was George Spira's voice. "Hansen? You here?"

Hansen went out. Spira sat on a desk.

"You've heard?" the developer said.

"I heard. You think it was those Perkinses?"

"The Perkinses?" Spira said.

"I heard Stewart had dug up some dirt on them."

"You don't think Charley Tucker's involved?"

"Tucker?" Hansen said.

Neither of them moved in the sunny office, yet there was an aura of two cats circling in the room, wary.

"You didn't talk to Hoag or Lee Beckett?" Spira said. "Then how'd you know Stewart was dead? Where the hell were you last night?"

"I was right here. Where were you?" Hansen lit a cigarette, smoked. "Bill Mackay told us."

"Where is he? I want to talk to him. Why did he come to tell you—" Spira stopped. *Us?*

Hansen walked into his private rooms. For a moment, Spira didn't move. Then he followed. From the bedroom doorway he saw Barbara Stewart still lying on the bed.

"Did Stewart know?" Spira said.

Her eyes were closed. "He knew."

"But you two were here all night? Together. That's your story? An alibi for each other."

"She doesn't need an alibi," Hansen said.

"That kind of marriage, Stewart and her?" Spira said. "How about you? Maybe you had some plans."

"Lay off, you hear?" Hansen said. "You had more to gain from stopping the Perkins trial than anyone!"

"I wonder," Spira said. "Tell me where I can find Mackay."

"I don't know," Barbara said. "I don't care."

"Spira," Hansen said, "why not let the police talk to Mackay and anyone else? Let the police handle it all."

"Lie low and sweep it under the rug? Hope everything will just go away? Back to business as usual?"

"Isn't that what we all want?" Hansen said.

*

Headquarters for the Eller for Attorney General campaign was a store just off Fremont's main street. The campaign manager glanced around the long, busy room.

"Mackay? Yes, there he is. Come on back."

Beckett followed the manager to the rear where Bill Mackay, a short, muscular young man, bent over a mimeograph machine.

"Guy from the County Prosecutor to see you," the manager said, and grinned to Beckett. "Tell Charley Tucker we'll whup him."

Mackay looked up from his machine, his eyes full of question over his heavy mustache.

"You don't have to be surprised," Beckett said. "I've talked to Maxwell Bowman."

Mackay returned to his machine.

"Who found him?"

"Tucker."

Mackay looked up again. He smiled. "How about that! Out at the house to make some deal? Beautiful."

"What were you out at the house to do?"

"Visit my parents."

"Before six-thirty in the morning?"

"Do I tell you when to go home?"

"A dutiful son who loved his stepfather?"

"We hated each other's guts," Mackay said cheerfully, worked on his mimeograph. "What do you want, Beckett?"

"You discovered a murder, failed to report it. Why?"

"I found my stepfather dead in his bed. I'm not a cop, I don't decide how or why he died, and I had some things to do before I notified anyone."

"Like talk to Maxwell Bowman?"

"And my mother. I thought she ought to know."

"Where is she?"

"Phil Hansen's office. He's got rooms behind the office, they're an item, eh? There all last night, if you wondered."

"Why go to Bowman first? To give him the good news?"

Mackay laughed. "You could say that. He's paying me to help stop that house, I figured I owed him first report."

"Is that all you did for him? Report?"

"You mean did I kill Gordon?"

"You could have."

"Don't push me around, Beckett. I can take care of myself in every way. Maybe I did kill him, but you'll have to prove it before you get tough with me or you could get hurt!"

"A threat, Mackay?"

"Cops don't make me tremble, I know my rights."

"If you did it, I'll prove it."

Mackay bent over his mimeograph again. "That might not be an easy job."

*

Barbara Stewart paced the bedroom behind the real estate office.

"I just can't go home, Phil! Do you understand?"

"Sure, Barb," Hansen nodded. "Empty house, bad vibes, it'd shake me up too, but you've got to take hold, keep going. You've got to build a new life, a future. Life has to go on. You—"

"Oh God, TV philosophy. You don't understand me at all." She watched Hansen, then reached to touch his face. "I'm sorry. I knew all that from the start, why should I blame you for being what you are? I don't even understand myself."

Hansen held her hand. "You've got to go home, Barb. It's going to start looking funny soon."

"I can't face it!" She pulled her hand away. "The eyes, the questions, the telephone calls to the bereaved widow."

"Look, Mackay and his family are coming to stay awhile, right? Mackay can handle all that for you."

She sat down on the bed. "I forgot. She fawns over him like a dog, accepts any filthy thing he does. The children are half animals and half robots." She shuddered. "I hate him. Where did he come from? Is he my son?"

60

"That's your trouble." Hansen grinned. "You're too young to have a son his age. Makes you think you're older than you feel, gets you down."

"Is that my trouble, Phil?"

"That's it, and I know how to fix it." He lay down behind her on the bed, pulled her down beside him. Playful.

She watched him. "And you have what I need."

"Come on, you'll feel ready to face dragons."

She broke away from his bear hug, stood up. "All right, you can take me home, Phil."

Hansen jumped off the bed. He was angry.

"I was just trying to cheer you up. Calm you down, damn it."

"My dragons aren't so easily faced."

She went out to Hansen's car. The real estate man locked the office and got into the driver's seat.

"We better talk to Krankl before I take you down to Cuyama. The Torres sales goes into escrow tomorrow."

He drove through the residential back streets to an area of older houses near the harbor, and parked in the driveway of a frame bungalow with a postage-stamp front lawn and a large mobile-home cruiser parked at the rear.

"I'll stay in the car," Barbara said.

A short man with thin brown hair and steel-rimmed glasses came out of the house. He peered toward the car.

"That Barbara? She's taking it hard? The husband?"

"Let's get the work done, Oscar," Hansen said.

"They know who did it yet? Why?" Oscar Krankl said.

"I don't know."

"And I don't like it all," Krankl said. "Not one damn."

"Who does?"

The two men went on into the small house. In the car, Barbara Stewart sat looking out at the quiet street.

*

Beckett looked out the living room window of the two-story colonial house. The cube house was less domineering here, but it still stood out bold and square beyond Bowman's house.

"So you were hunting over on the other side of Dresden," Beckett said, "and Mrs. Hillock was at home? Anyone see you?"

"No," Patricia Hillock said, "if that's your business."

She was a bony woman in her early fifties, wearing a slim blue dress. Her blond hair was short and bleached, and she had the impatient face of someone accustomed to power over subordinates. A commander's wife. Colonel Hillock was the commander—firm and direct, but a little less sure of himself.

"Not even a dead pig for proof," Hillock said. "We didn't kill Stewart, Beckett, but we're not sorry about it. To my mind he was a sharp lawyer defending people who don't belong in this community. Working against his own people."

"And you only bought this house six months ago," Beckett said. "A big investment at today's prices."

"We don't have to listen to innuendo," Patricia Hillock snapped. "Arrest us or get out. Right now!"

"If you remember anyone who can support your alibis," Beckett said, "I'd like you to get in touch."

Patricia Hillock stood at the front window and watched Beckett drive away. Her face was pinched.

"I don't like that man around," she said. "The kind who noses into everything. We don't want that, do we? We don't want him to know that Casey was up here last night from your old command. You really better go down and talk to Casey, find out for sure what's going on."

Hillock nodded.

8

The office of the Buena Costa County Prosecutor is on the second floor of the old brick courthouse in San Vicente. Built by the Americans after the Mexican War when all things Spanish were inferior, the courthouse has resisted the modern homage to Spanish architecture if not to "Spanish" people.

Lee Beckett sat in Tucker's office and reported his day.

"I hope you've come up with an alibi, Charley."

"Home in bed, if that's an alibi. He died around three A.M."

"As good as most. No one has a real alibi."

"Par for that time of night. Everyone in bed."

"Not everyone. Mackay, Maxwell Bowman, Colonel Hillock, and Cathy Perkins were up or could have been. Most of the rest too." Beckett shook his head. "The cube house isn't enough, Charley. I'd swear to that. Except maybe for Bill Mackay, none of them are people who'd kill over that house alone. There's got to be more."

"The 'personal business' of Cathy Perkins?" Tucker said.

"Maybe." Beckett thought. "Stewart's secretary won't let me look at his files. I'll need a warrant, Charley."

"First thing tomorrow."

Beckett rubbed at his face. "Mackay says Barbara Stewart and Phil Hansen are swinging an affair, and someone was out in the trees watching that house." He showed Tucker the brass disk. "I found that in the trees across Beacon Road."

Tucker examined the disk. "Barbara Stewart has money. Three hundred thousand or so from her father. Her first husband, Mackay's father, is back in town. An oddball who quit work five years ago to go sailing a boat."

Beckett looked out at the palms. "Something's missing, Charley. I'm pretty sure it wasn't suicide, I don't see how he could have done it by accident, but it's a funny way to murder."

*

Sweat poured down Bill Mackay's naked body as he sat in the sauna at the Tennis Club. He didn't move when Maxwell Bowman and George Spira came in draped in towels.

"Mackay? This is George Spira," Bowman said. He dropped his towel, sat on the bench. "He wants to talk. He's the—"

"I know who Mr. Spira is," Mackay said. He smiled at the two naked older men as if comparing their bodies to his. The comparison seemed to please him.

"The police are hinting you did more than find Stewart dead," Spira said.

"Are they?" Mackay closed his eyes.

Spira mopped the sweat from his thick body as he watched the unmoving younger man. Bowman breathed hard in the stifling heat, flabby and uneasy.

"I didn't hire you to murder anyone!" Bowman said.

"You hired me to do a job." Mackay's voice was scornful. "You didn't ask how I'd do it, and I didn't say how I'd do it."

"Then I'm firing you!" Bowman said.

Mackay opened his eyes. He didn't change his position, or wipe the sweat from his body. He had contempt in his eyes.

"Don't be a weakling, Bowman. I despise weak men. You hired me to get something done, and I'm doing what I think is necessary to get it done. Whatever I did you're already part of it. You made a decision, stick to it like a man."

"Did you kill him, Mackay?" Spira said.

Mackay smiled. "You have more to lose than anyone, maybe you killed him. Or Bowman himself. I had the feeling that he was already up when I called this morning."

"That's a lie!" Bowman was pale in the airless heat.

"I'd respect you if you did. Or Spira there. I admire men with the guts to know what they want and the will to do something about it."

Spira said, "So do I, but I admire some intelligence too. Killing Stewart was a stupid play, it won't end anything. A postponement, nothing more."

"You never know. It might make some people think," Mackay said. "But maybe none of us did it. Gordon had found out something about the Perkinses. He was coming around to our side. If we didn't have much to gain, maybe they did."

"Can you prove that?" Spira said.

"I think so. We'll have to wait and see."

Mackay closed his eyes again, began to move his muscles in yoga exercises.

*

Sheriff Hoag nodded when Beckett finished explaining what he had learned that day.

"Yeh, we don't have anything solid either. Not a clue out there; the labs came up empty. It looks like a long one."

"You sound like that's okay with you. Keep Charley Tucker in hot water as long as possible? Maybe you don't want to solve it."

"I didn't hear that, Beckett."

"You're sure you care about Stewart being dead?"

"I'm not all broken up," Hoag said. "But we'll handle it. I'm not so sure he was a big loss to the community."

Beckett leaned back in his chair. Hoag was probably right about the community, the proper establishment community, and the police were on the side of the community. The Perkinses were radical troublemakers, the lawyer who defended them had not been loved, and the police are human.

"You saw where someone had been watching the Stewart house from across the road?"

"Hell, it could have been anyone from a neighbor to a vagrant. We're checking neighbors, questioning all vagrants."

"What about where it looks like someone was lying in the weeds near the garage?"

"Could have been a dog. We found no clues."

"Mrs. Stewart's affair with Hansen? Her money?"

"We'll talk to everyone, investigate everything, and let the chips fall."

"The longer you take, the more they fall around Tucker."

"You know how small my staff is," Hoag said.

"Sure," Beckett said. "Take it slow, Sheriff."

*

Barbara Stewart stood in the gravel of the driveway in front of the big house in Cuyama Beach. The evening sunlight slanted through the trees like the planes of a cubist painting. She stood there for some time, looking at the overgrown brush and neglected flower beds.

She went into the house and listened to the silence. She looked at herself in the hallway mirror. Her tanned face was gaunt under the smooth blond hair. Her eyes like flat silver coins. She still wore the gray pantsuit she had put on over a hundred years ago last night.

Room by room she walked through the cool, hushed old house. Walked but didn't look, seemed only to listen to the empty rooms. Until she stood again, as she had last night, at the second floor hall window and looked out toward the garage.

A shape seemed to move among the trees beyond the garage. A shadow. Barbara shivered.

Her hand moved as if remembering something. She looked down at her hand. Then she went down into the kitchen where the bottle and glass still stood on the kitchen table. At the refrigerator she got ice, poured a drink, and sat down in the silent kitchen to drink the whisky. When the glass was empty she got up.

She walked out of the house and across the ragged grounds under the trees to the garage. She put her hand on the railing of the outside stairs and looked up. The apartment door above was partly open. She went up. Inside the small apartment she stood over the bed.

No blood, no violence, only the unmade bed as if someone had just gotten up.

"Did you kill him?"

The voice was behind her, in the doorway. A nice voice, deep and quiet.

"Yes," she said. "I killed him."

She heard the man move closer, come into the room.

"You weren't with Hansen all night?"

"Yes, I was with Phil all night." She turned. "That's how I killed him, you see? With Phil while he was here alone."

Beckett studied her. He began to walk around the room, inspecting various small objects.

"Where did you go with Hansen? When?"

She had gone back to looking down at the bed. She reached out and touched it. Then she seemed to hear Beckett's question, looked away from the bed and out the apartment window toward the big white house.

"He picked me up late. We had a few drinks. We went to his rooms behind the office."

"Anyone see you having drinks?"

"I don't know." She moved her head back and forth as if shaking away a fly.

"Anyone see Hansen pick you up here? Late?"

"Here?" She went on looking out the window at her house beyond the trees. "Yes. Gordon saw Phil pick me up."

Beckett stopped his slow tour of the room, and turned to face her. She was no longer looking out the window. She was looking at him, her head tilted back, defiant. Then she looked down again at the bed, touched it, and lay down. Stretched rigid on her back, her hands folded across her stomach in the gray suit.

"You're saying you killed Stewart by having the affair with Hansen? You mean you think it was suicide?"

She laughed. Her eyes were wet. "Poor Gordon."

"Why would he change cars? For suicide?"

"I killed them all, the men. My own way. They killed me."

Beckett moved closer. "Are you ill, Mrs. Stewart?"

"Ill? No. Sick, perhaps, not ill."

Her body rigid on the unmade bed, she moved her head back and forth like someone trying to escape an iron lung.

68

Beckett sat down in an easy chair facing the bed.

"I'm sorry I have to ask questions. You want a doctor?"

"No. Are you a policeman?"

"Lee Beckett, County Prosecutor's Office," he said. He waited, but she said nothing more. "I don't think it was suicide, Mrs. Stewart. His actions don't add up."

"No, I suppose not."

"Hansen was with you all night?"

"Yes."

"Who would want your husband dead? Can you think of a motive?"

"No motive. No one."

"An enemy?"

"He had no enemies," she said. "Only me."

"Your marriage wasn't a good one?"

She watched the ceiling above the bed. She smiled. "As good as most, I expect, perhaps. For me. For him, too, I expect. Maybe. I don't know. I—" she trailed off, vague.

"You work with Hansen too, right? You're involved in the cube house hassle? Could that have been the motive?"

"Possibly." She took a sudden deep breath and her rigid body seemed to relax. Her voice grew stronger. "Yes, I suppose it could have been."

"Which side?"

"Side? Either. Ours or his."

"Was he going to quit the case?"

"He said nothing to me. My son says he was, but my son would say anything that suited him, suited his purposes. I don't like my son, Mr. Beckett. Gordon didn't like my son. His father doesn't like my son!"

"Your first husband is in Fremont?"

"Yes."

"Who gets your money now?"

"Money? You mean what my father left me? It's mine,

69

no one gets it until . . . Oh, I see. William, I suppose, eventually." She turned to look at Beckett. "My God, what a world this is! You mean you think someone might have killed Gordon so that eventually they would get the money and not Gordon. William? Tom McKay? What a filthy world!"

"It's our world, good and bad. How do you get along with your first husband?"

"I haven't seen Tom in five years, and not really for almost twenty years. I . . . No, wait." She lay there studying the ceiling again. "I forgot. All this . . . I saw him only yesterday. Yes. I went to see him on his boat. He was nice, friendly, we talked of sailing away together. The South Seas. Is that always the way, Mr. Beckett? Twenty years later you can be nice to each other?"

"He wanted to sail off with you? Together?"

She didn't answer, seemed to be seeing her first husband and the South Seas on the bare ceiling.

"Now I can," she said. "That's what you're thinking, isn't it? If I wanted to, now I could. If Tom wanted to."

"It's a thought," Beckett said. "I've got my job."

She looked at him. "And that's important, isn't it? Your job. Your duty. Saves you having to think of good and bad." She stared up at nothing again. "Have you finished your job here? For now?"

"Unless you have anything else to tell me."

She shook her head, went on staring up at the ceiling.

9

The black ball flashed in the four-walled-handball court. Naked to the waist, the two men played hard and in silence, a grim struggle without quarter. They powered the hard ball and outmaneuvered each other. The taller man finally won.

"Too good for me, Greg," Bill Mackay said.

"Only on a handball court," the tall man said.

A Tennis Club attendant appeared. "Mr. Mackay? Telephone. You can take it in the locker room."

Toweling his face and neck, his eyes still bright with the action of the game, Bill Mackay picked up the receiver in the steamy locker room.

"Bill?" the voice at the other end said. "Jesse Eller. What the hell's going on down there?"

"Hi, Senator. Where are you? Something wrong?"

"I'm in Sacramento, of course, and you tell me if something's wrong. What's all this about you and a murdered lawyer? Your stepfather?"

Bill Mackay glanced slowly around the empty locker room. He sat down on a bench. His voice was low.

"He was killed last night. No one knows yet who did it,

as far as I know, but he was defending some people who built a crazy avant-garde–type house in a nice development with an architectural covenant and the community is suing to have it torn down. It's all good for us, Senator."

"Good?" Eller was silent at the other end. "How?"

"I figure the whole cube house mess is just the kind of issue we needed, locally here and maybe across the whole state. It's got the community up in arms, and Charley Tucker's caught right in the middle. We're solid for the community and the right to have those covenants; Tucker's liberal backers are for the people who built the house, but he knows he can't win with the liberals alone. To top it off, Tucker found the body, and Hoag's making the most of it in the newspapers."

Another silence. "Good God, you don't really think that Tucker could have killed that man?"

"Maybe not, but he wasn't out there at eight in the morning for a social call. He had to be trying to make a deal with my stepfather to play down the cube house case, maybe even trying to force a compromise to close it out. It looks nice and bad—County Prosecutor trying to influence a civil case for political advantage!"

"That's all there is?" Senator Eller said.

"What else?"

"I heard that *you* really found the body first."

Mackay frowned in the empty locker room. "Who told you that, Senator?"

"You're not the only man I have down there."

"Okay, I found him. It's my home. I wanted to tell my mother before I reported it. I've got it all under control."

Eller was silent once more. "I hope so."

The Senator hung up. Mackay continued to towel off in the silent locker room. Then he began to dress quickly.

*

In his Sacramento office, Senator Jesse Eller stared down at his telephone for a time. Then he bent to his intercom.

"Get me on a flight to San Vicente. Yes, right now. If you can't find a commercial flight, charter one."

*

Cathy Perkins hurried along the dark breakwater, the spray misting her face and making the uneven stone walkway slick. Ahead, the quick-eyed young man in flared blue cords and a dark red quilted jacket leaned on the stone parapet and watched a big yawl round the end of the breakwater and bury its nose in white water as it breasted the open sea.

"You've heard about Mr. Stewart?" Cathy said.

"Yeh," the young man said. "You didn't do it, did you?"

"You think I did!"

Outraged, she stared at him. He watched the lights of the yawl move on out to sea, the boat heeled far over.

"Then it's perfect. A great development," he said.

"You don't care about people at all, do you?"

He straightened up. "People are all I care about—what they think, believe, want. What they want is violence, blood—especially if the other side does it. They can be outraged then, and still enjoy the thrill. Tell me everything going on."

"All I know is that Mr. Stewart is dead, a man named Mackay is telling everyone that he was going to quit our case because we were up to something unethical, and an investigator named Beckett has talked to both John and me. I'm scared."

"Bill Mackay," the young man said. "Senator Eller's hatchet man. Maybe he spotted us meeting. Was Stewart going to quit?"

"No." Cathy hesitated. "But he did talk about it."

"So?" He watched the now distant running lights of the yawl. "Where's your husband tonight?"

73

"He went to his office."

"Okay. I'll try to keep an eye on Mackay and dig some more into the Mar Vista gang. I want to look into that Phil Hansen who sold you the lot, and Stewart's wife who works with him. There could be an angle there."

Cathy looked down to where the breakers hit the rocks below. "Perhaps we should stop. Someone murdered Mr. Stewart."

"Risk in everything," the young man said cheerfully, "and a murder always helps. To top it off, it looks like one of the Mar Vista crew has some other little problem—that Colonel Hillock. I think we're going to do fine."

*

Beckett had stopped for dinner at a sea food restaurant across the shore drive from the harbor. Now he drove toward John Perkins's office on the downtown side street. He wanted to find out if Gordon Stewart had ever talked about his wife and Phil Hansen to his client. Or if Hansen had said anything about Stewart.

The two-story gray frame house two blocks from downtown had been renovated into small offices. The directory showed that John Perkins, Architect, had his office on the ground floor at the rear.

Beckett heard the sounds as he reached the door.

A low, heavy breathing inside the office. Like the panting of some animal.

And a slow sound of dragging, of something that moved against wood and metal. The rustling of paper.

Beckett drew his gun, opened the office door.

The dark office was a chaos of pulled-out drawers, opened filing cabinets, overturned chairs, and scattered heaps of papers—plans, contracts, magazines, drawings, and all the other contents of crowded files.

John Perkins moved on the floor. There was blood, and the heavyset young architect was crawling slowly through the debris as if trying to see if anything was gone. His eyes were glazed, he breathed slow and heavy, and his movements were more reflex than conscious.

Beckett bent over him, stopped his almost aimless crawling. Perkins looked up, only half aware of Beckett, and saying nothing. He had been shot in the shoulder by some big gun. It looked like a clean wound, through the flesh not bone. He had lost blood, and shock was thick behind the glazed eyes.

Beckett called the paramedics, found a towel in the small bathroom of the office, wet it, and kneeled beside the wounded man wiping his face with the cool cloth. Perkins watched him the way a dog watches its master, breathing slowly now, not trying to speak. The paramedics arrived.

While they worked on Perkins, Beckett examined the searched office. The outer door had been opened with a picklock. A neat job, almost professional. The first blood was just inside the door. Beckett found no ejected shell in the room.

He rode with the paramedics to St. Stephen's Hospital. As the doctors worked on John Perkins, he called Sheriff Hoag and reported what had happened. He couldn't tell Hoag anything more until he talked to Perkins. It was nearly midnight when the doctor came out. "No real damage, the bullet went through cleanly. He's weak, but you can see him briefly."

Perkins lay flat in the bed, his shoulder thick with bandages. His eyes were still glazed, but the shock was gone.

"I opened my door, saw the mess, and then I was knocked over. I . . . flung down. Some noise, loud, and warm liquid. Pain . . . later."

"Did you see him?" Beckett asked.

"No." Perkins moved his head. "What . . . did he want?"

"What did you have?"

"No money. No . . . My work . . . That's all." Perkins seemed to be trying to remember something. "Shadow . . . I saw the shadow . . . go out . . . nothing . . . in his hands!"

"He didn't find what he wanted. Or could remember it."

Perkins closed his eyes. "My wife?"

"Coming. She wasn't home, but she's on her way now."

Perkins smiled.

*

The night watchman unlocked the side door of the courthouse.

"Overtime, Mr. Beckett?"

"No rest, Eddie."

Beckett went up to his office. The wide corridor echoed hollowly to his footsteps. He turned on his light, sat down at his desk, and heard the noise.

In Tucker's office next door. He drew his pistol again, moved silently to the connecting door.

Tucker's office was empty—with the desk light on, papers scattered, and the window open.

Below on the dark courthouse grounds a figure seemed to move among the palms and shadows. Beckett called Tucker.

In his own office he wrote his daily report while he waited. Tucker arrived in ten minutes.

"One man, came in through the window," Beckett said.

Tucker checked his desk and files. It took half an hour.

"Nothing missing, Lee. As far as I can tell he only searched my desk and my personal file."

"Two searches, nothing missing," Beckett said. "Looking for dirt, Charley? Some angle to use for something?''

"Or wanted to know how we're doing on some case?''

"Maybe.'' Beckett said. "We better sleep on it.''

*

Night settled over Fremont. A tower clock struck two.

In the building around the corner from Fremont's main street, a figure slipped inside Gordon Stewart's office. There was a faint scraping of metal, the click of a lock opening. A drawer rasped on its metal and plastic runners.

Five minutes later the figure left the office. Out on the empty side street a car started, drove away.

The night became silent again.

10

Beckett slept poorly. Something loomed all night in his mind just out of reach. At dawn he was wide awake. He got up, worked for an hour in his greenhouses, then had breakfast.

He studied the small brass disk. An old-fashioned hotel key tag? From some small, perhaps remote, hotel?

He finished his coffee, checked his pistol, and went to his car. He took the freeway out of San Vicente to Fremont again. There was no one home at George Spira's big house. He drove on to Spira's office. Spira wasn't there. The secretary smiled.

"Tennis Club poker game last night," she said.

Would-be champions were already on the courts of the Tennis Club, and up in the game room six men still sat at the green table.

"I call you, Oscar," George Spira said.

"Flush," Oscar Krankl said. "Ace-king."

"Beats me," Spira said.

"Full boat, jacks and tens," Colonel Benjamin Hillock said.

"Shit," Oscar Krankl said.

Beckett stood at the rear of the room isolated from the distant thud of tennis balls and the faint splashing in the pool. A club waiter came in with coffee. Beckett spoke to him. He set the coffee on a sideboard hot plate and leaned down to George Spira. Spira took another card, checked his down cards, tossed the hand in, and got up.

"I wondered when you'd get around to me."

"I figured Hoag would get to you. Didn't he?"

"He did. Let's go out on the balcony."

The open balcony encircled the second floor of the building overlooking the courts. More players had arrived, all wearing tailored tennis outfits the colors of the rainbow and carrying the best racquets. For most of them, as Beckett watched, their games weren't in a class with their equipment.

"Profitable game?" Beckett said.

"Useful." The developer smiled. "Bank loan officers, FHA men, private investors. High stakes, and a good loser makes friends. Comes time for business—good old George. Any progress?"

"What did Hoag tell you?"

"He's not in my pocket, Beckett, and I'm not part of his team. All I know is that Stewart's dead, and Hoag suggested I make sure my Mar Vista people have alibis."

"None of them do. Neither do the Perkinses or Bill Mackay. Hansen and Stewart's widow only alibi each other."

"And neither do I," Spira said. "We all have the cube house for a motive. Property values, politics, or both."

Beckett leaned on the balcony railing. He watched a girl whose bright red pants flashed under her short pink skirt each time she hit the ball.

"Back in New York I once heard the Commissioner give a speech about what detective work was really like. First it was ninety percent slogging and paperwork—searching the files and mug books, reading lab reports, ringing doorbells, using the computer. That's because ninety percent of major crimes are done by criminals. In nine of the remaining ten percent it's a matter of plodding from clue to clue, step to step."

The girl didn't play very well, but she looked nice.

"Now and then it's none of that, the last one percent and mostly white-collar crimes. The files and computers don't help, no one involved is in them, and there aren't any real clues."

Spira seemed to be watching the girl in the red pants too.

"And this is one of those?" he said.

Beckett nodded. "We've got a button the victim himself could have had as easily as anyone, no other physical evidence, and no fingerprints that can't be explained. Mackay's, Charley Tucker's, Barbara Stewart's in the apartment. Stewart's own, Barbara's, and Phil Hansen's on the Cadillac—but Barbara and Hansen work together, and the Caddy is what she drives for business. No blood, no weapon. Some footprints that could belong to any vagrant. A spot in the weeds that could be anything from the murderer to a dog. No one has an alibi, but no one was seen near the Stewart house either."

The girl in the red pants made a point and jumped in joy.

"Where does that leave you?" Spira said.

"With the Commissioner's last two aspects of detective work—intuition and accident," Beckett said. "This is the kind of case that gets solved when someone makes a mistake later, or when we stumble across an unexpected clue or witness. That's what Hoag's doing—going around and around the same ground, looking through the hobo camps and bars for a chance witness, talking to everyone in Cuyama Beach. Maybe someone will come forward, or maybe we'll find a witness."

80

"If you don't?"

"Then it may never get solved," Beckett said. "If it's murder at all. We're still not sure of even that."

"And intuition?" Spira said. He watched the girl sprawl as she missed a passing shot. She had good legs. "You left that for last, right?"

The girl down on the court picked herself up, and seemed to become aware of being watched. She looked up to where they leaned on the balcony rail, her expression half annoyed and half coy. Beckett didn't look away or change expression.

"I don't think the cube house is a good enough motive," he said. "Not for murder."

"What is a good enough motive?"

"Maybe something private, personal. Barbara Stewart has some money, Stewart could have been in the way of someone who wants it—now or later. Then there's her affair with Hansen."

"They say Stewart knew about it."

"Maybe he didn't accept it, had plans," Beckett said. "Or maybe one of them wanted it to be more than an affair."

"Hansen has a wife," Spira said.

The girl below was playing self-consciously now, aware of them watching her. They walked away along the open balcony.

"What else?" Spira said. "You've got more on your mind."

"The cube house isn't a good enough motive—not alone. I don't see it as the motive by itself. But there could be another motive, another problem, connected to it that is big enough. Something that ties into the cube house, directly or indirectly."

Spira nodded slowly, but he said nothing.

"Perkins's office was broken into," Beckett said. "So was Tucker's. You know anything about that? Who or why?"

"No," Spira said.

"And you have no ideas to offer about Stewart's death?"

"No."

"If you get any ideas, you'll give me a call?"

"I'll call," Spira said.

Beckett left the balcony and walked out to his car. Spira watched him go.

*

Bill Mackay turned into the driveway of the big white house on Beacon Road and saw the station wagon parked there. He parked behind the dusty wagon, and strode into the house. A young woman no more than twenty-five yet somehow matronly, and inches taller than Mackay, hurried out of the living room to meet him. Her small face was agitated.

"Bill! What do they mean? Your father dead? Where's your mother? A sheriff's deputy was here looking for you!"

"Calm down, Grace!" Mackay snapped. "Damn it, haven't I taught you anything?"

She flinched as if slapped. "Yes, I'm sorry, dear."

"That's better."

Grace Mackay folded her hands in front of her. She wore no makeup, and that, with her cheap and old-fashioned print dress and severe brown hair tied back in a bun, gave her the matronly look. But her blue eyes were young and seemed to wait for what Mackay would say next.

"My *stepfather* was killed two nights ago. The police are investigating. What did you tell the deputy?"

"That I didn't know where you were. Killed? You mean someone . . . murdered him? Here?"

"That's how it looks. Barbara isn't home?"

82

"No. Do you think we should stay somewhere else?"

"It's my home," Mackay said. He laughed. "It'll be all mine someday for sure now, we might as well get used to it."

"Yes, all right," Grace said. "How . . . how is the campaign going here?"

"Okay. It looks good, but there's something more important going on. You and the kids get settled and—"

"More important? Work for the Senator?"

"You know better than to ask that; I'll handle my work. Just get moved in. We can use three of the bedrooms. Where are the kids?"

"In the yard. They were so cooped up on the trip."

Mackay walked through the house to the back door from the kitchen. He stood in the open door and whistled loudly. Two boys and a girl came running from the yard. Three, four, and five, they crowded around their father. He smiled, patted each of them, then stepped back and studied them critically.

"All right, now get your things up to your rooms, and wash up. Then you can do your lessons so you won't be behind in school when you go home. March now."

The children hurried away, and Mackay turned to his wife.

"Check out the kitchen, I'll be home for dinner. If my plans change, I'll try to call."

"Yes, Bill," Grace Mackay said.

*

The door of the Hansen Realty bungalow in the side street was locked. Hansen's home address was on the door. Beckett returned to his car. The address was in the suburbs between Fremont and Cuyama Beach.

The house was an ugly imitation Tudor of white plaster and fake half timbers from the time before World War II when houses in California still wanted to look Eastern. The kind of ungainly house a real estate man lives in when he can't sell it to anyone else.

Hansen himself answered the door. The handsome, athletic-looking real estate man glanced quickly over his shoulder when he saw Beckett.

"Couldn't you go to my office, Beckett?"

"I went to your office."

A woman's voice called, "Who is it, Phil?"

"Just a guy to see me, Ann," Hansen called back. In a lower voice, "Come on into the den."

As Beckett followed him inside, a short blond woman who looked ten years older than Hansen appeared from the living room. She stared at Beckett.

"Lee Beckett, Mrs. Hansen. Prosecutor's Office."

"Why not use the living room, Phil?" she said.

"All right, the living room," Hansen said. "You kids get out of here."

Surlily, a boy and girl in their early teens left the living room TV set. Large and messy, it was the room of a poor housekeeper whose husband wasn't home much.

"Some coffee, Mr. Beckett?" Ann Hansen asked.

"No, thank you. Can we talk in private, Hansen?"

"I have nothing to hide from my wife."

"Then tell me about Wednesday night."

"I had to go up to Monteverde to talk to a seller, it got so late I decided to stay up there in a motel." Hansen's voice was steady, but his eyes were pleading.

"I will have that coffee, Mrs. Hansen," Beckett said.

Ann Hansen left the room. Hansen wiped at his face.

"Thanks. Okay, I was with Barbara Stewart all night Wednesday. After about midnight, a little later maybe."

"Why so late?"

"She waited until Stewart was in bed."

84

"And that's your alibi?"

"I don't need an alibi. I had no reason to kill Stewart."

"Maybe Barbara Stewart did. You're sure she was with you?"

Hansen licked his lips. "She was with me."

"Did she talk about her first husband? Her son? Money?"

"No. I mean, not recently."

"Was Stewart giving her trouble about you?"

"No!"

"Did she have any business troubles?"

"No."

"And she was with you all night? Be real sure, Hansen."

"I said she was, didn't I?"

Beckett walked out of the shabby house.

*

Ann Hansen stood in the doorway between the dining room and the living room. She held the cup of coffee, listened to Beckett's car drive away.

"That man has ideas, Phil."

Hansen whirled. "How long were you—?"

"He's suspicious of you, or Barbara, or both," Ann said. "And don't worry about what I heard. I knew about you and Barbara. I know about all your women. I always have."

"I don't know what the hell you're—"

She put the cup down hard. Coffee sloshed onto the table. She ignored it. "I don't care about your women; I haven't for years. But I care about your business. I care that you go on working and making lots of money. I'm glad you were with Barbara that night. At least it gives you an alibi."

"Now, look, you're all wrong—"

"Oh, shut up! You don't care about me, and I don't care about you! But I'm stuck with you. What happens to you,

85

happens to me. That's the way it is in this world, and I want all I can get for myself and the kids. I want you to make lots of money. So I'll back you all the way, but you better never let me down! You're sure you were with Barbara *all* that night?"

Hansen hesitated, then shrugged. "All night."

"Like the man just said, you better be sure. You're not going to protect Barbara at my expense. You understand that?"

They faced each other in the shabby living room. Hansen nodded.

11

Grace Mackay looked up from preparing her pork roast. Barbara Stewart watched her from the kitchen doorway. The new widow seemed to be studying Grace, interested but curious at the same time. Grace hurried to her.

"Oh, Barbara, how terrible for you!"

"Terrible?" Barbara seemed interested in the word. "I don't know. For Gordon perhaps. I'm not even sure of that."

Grace dried her hands. "I don't care what you pretend, it must be dreadful for you. I don't think I could go on. I wouldn't want to live."

"Throw yourself on his funeral pyre? Take poison? The faithful and devoted wife?"

Grace went back to her roast, bent over it working. Barbara sat at the kitchen table. She watched her daughter-in-law as if she were looking at a far-off landscape.

"You loved Mr. Stewart," Grace said. "I know that."

"I'm sorry he's dead, Grace," Barbara said. "I feel sad, very sad. Is that good enough for you?"

"Of course you do! But we'll all help."

"Thank you."

Grace rubbed pepper into the roast. "Do they know who could have done it? Bill didn't say."

"I don't think so, not yet. They will, I expect. Not that that will change anything."

"It would for me! I'd want him to suffer the way he'd made me suffer. I'd want him to die!"

"What makes you sure it was a him?"

"A woman?" Grace stared at Barbara. "Why would a woman kill him? I mean, it was his work, wasn't it? Business?"

"Is that coffee on the stove?" Barbara stood, poured a cup of coffee, sat down again. "A roast on Friday?"

"Bill's been alone, he'll enjoy a good dinner."

"I'm sure he will."

"He may not get home for dinner, but it'll be ready when he does."

Barbara sipped her coffee. It was hot, the steam seemed to bother her eyes. She closed them.

"Are you really happy, Grace? With a man like William?"

Grace scored the roast. "Why don't you like Bill?"

"He's not my kind of person."

"He's a fine man! A real man! I like a man to be a man. Any real woman does. He's strong, and smart, and someday he'll be great. He has a wonderful future."

"What about you? Your future?"

"I told you. We have a wonderful future."

Barbara went on sipping the coffee, her eyes closed in the big, quiet kitchen of the old house.

"You don't care what future? What he does? How he does it? You accept whatever he thinks and does?"

"Accept? I don't know what you mean, Barbara."

"No, I suppose you don't. Perhaps you're lucky."

Grace put the roast into its pan. "Sometimes I can't believe you're really Bill's mother."

"Neither can I," Barbara said, her eyes still closed, drinking the hot coffee.

*

At the harbormaster's office Beckett got the slip number of Tom McKay's sloop *Paloma*. It stood silent against the long dock in the clear October morning sun. A forty-footer streaked with rust, its paint peeling, the furled sails patched and dirty, its hull and gear battered from months at sea.

No one was on deck as Beckett climbed aboard. Then a head emerged from the main cabin hatchway. A broad, balding man burned the color of saddle leather. From his lined face and rough hands he was in his early sixties, but his voice and eyes were those of a younger man.

"Hello! Can I help?"

"Tom McKay?"

"Right, come on below. Coffee?"

The cabin was crammed with the needs of a boat that stayed long at sea. In the galley were the remains of a solitary breakfast and coffee on the stove. McKay poured Beckett a cup.

"You spell it Mc-K-a-y? Not Mackay?"

"You've met my storm trooper son? His symbol of rejection, independence, or defiance, I've never been sure which. A hollow gesture anyway, since I disowned the young punk years ago." McKay drank his coffee. "Which was an equally hollow gesture since his mother took him from me twenty-odd years ago." McKay laughed.

"Have you talked to him since he's been in town?"

"No, thank God! We have nothing to talk about."

"But you've talked to your ex-wife."

"Ah?" McKay set his cup down. "You're a cop?"

"County Prosecutor's Office. Lee Beckett."

89

"Trying to bail the boss out, eh?" McKay shook his head. "Bad thing about Stewart. I always thought he was a good man. Cared about people and what was right."

"You knew him well?"

"No. First husbands don't usually get chummy with their successors in our world. Besides, I've been away a long time."

"You sailed to the South Seas alone?"

"Not then. I had a crew. I probably could sail her alone now, but then I was a total landlubber."

"What made you cut loose?"

McKay stretched his legs out, leaned back in the canvas chair. "I'd worked all my life, was as high as I was going to get in the company, had enough money and no ties. I got to thinking I'd like to experience the adventures I'd read about. I decided I wanted to wear out not rust out. I had a dream about the sea, two of my grandfathers had been sea captains, and about Tahiti. I'd always wanted to sail off there and have a drink at Quinn's Bar in Papeete. Both those grandfathers had been lost at sea, and I'd never even been on a sailboat, but I bought the *Paloma,* took some sailing lessons and a few trips out to the Channel Islands, finished a correspondence course in navigation, and headed west with a crew of kids."

He smiled and his eyes shined as he relived that first sail toward the setting sun. "After twenty-one days we reached Hawaii, hung around a while, made repairs and corrected mistakes, and set off for Tahiti. I got my drinks at Quinn's, saw all the island groups, met a lot of simple people who never heard of civilized 'pressures.' You know there are kids out there, even couples with children, who live day to day, make whatever they can, sail island to island as a way of life. I think I may just go back and join them."

"Why did you come home at all? Money?"

"Partly," McKay said. "They say that most kids will love even the meanest, rottenest parents. I suppose we all have a home we want to go back to once in a while."

"I guess so," Beckett said. "What did you and Barbara Stewart talk about on Wednesday?"

McKay got up to pour another cup of coffee. Beckett declined. McKay sat down again, stirred the coffee.

"Nothing special. Call it a little reunion."

"Your idea?"

"No, she came to see me. Why?"

"I wondered. Stewart was killed that night. How was she acting? Did she talk about Stewart? About any problems?"

"Nothing about Stewart or problems, and she seemed fine, normal. She was always the calm type, reserved. Not flamboyant like me. It was just a visit to an old friend."

Beckett said, "Do you want her back, McKay?"

"Back? You mean remarry? After over twenty years?"

"Sail away together to the South Seas."

McKay laughed again. "Told you that, did she? Call it friendly fantasy; I'm surprised she even noticed. Maybe after a lot of years it happens like that—reshape the past in the image of the present, the way it might have been. You don't think I was serious? Or that she would consider it serious?"

"I don't know on either," Beckett said. "Where were you Wednesday night?"

"Here, on the town, somewhere. I'm not sure."

"Who saw you?"

"You think I killed Stewart to get Barbara back?"

"It's a theory. Someone was watching the house that night."

"Then you better find out who it was."

Beckett got up. "And you better stay in town."

"I won't be going anywhere. Need to pick up a stake."

"Barbara Stewart has money."

"What her father left her? Now that's an idea," McKay said. "Come for a sail, you look like a man who'd enjoy it."

"I would," Beckett said. "Another time."

*

John Perkins sat propped in the hospital bed. He was working slowly on some sketches. He didn't see the short, muscular man with the dark mustache come in.

"Redesigning that horror house?" the man said.

"Working for a client. One who hasn't canceled. Who are you?"

"Bill Mackay."

"The one who's been lying about us?"

"Am I lying?"

"You know you are!"

Mackay sat down, tilted back in the chair. "Why don't you sell out? Get what you can and go somewhere else."

"I have no intention of selling."

"Matter of principle?"

"A matter of my own house how and where I want it," Perkins said. "No schemes and no crusades."

Mackay teetered in the chair, the creaking of the metal loud in the silent room. Mackay seemed to enjoy the sound.

"Gordon believed in principle," he said. "It looks like that can be dangerous."

"That sounds almost like a threat. Should I be afraid?"

"Call it friendly advice."

"I appreciate anything friendly," Perkins said. "But I think I like my house just where it is and as it is."

Mackay let the chair come down hard on its legs. "Too bad. Think about the options anyway. You already need a new lawyer, if you can get one. You've already been shot once."

Mackay got up. At the door he looked back.

92

"If you're so sure that what I told Gordon about you is a lie, why don't you talk to your wife? She might know something you don't."

Perkins said, "I doubt that, Mackay."

*

The Fremont House sat high on a bluff above the sea. George Spira found Phil Hansen and Oscar Krankl at lunch in the elegant dining room. Out in the channel the oil platforms stood out like distant aircraft carriers.

"You two didn't win this much money last night," Spira said as he joined them.

"Phil didn't play long enough last night to win a hamburger," Oscar Krankl said. "Well, back to work. When do we talk about the low-income housing project, George?"

"In a couple of weeks."

After Krankl had gone, Spira ordered a beer. He looked out toward the ocean and the oil platforms.

"Lee Beckett came to see me this morning," he said.

"He's out to protect Charley Tucker," Hansen said. "I don't like that guy, too narrow. A big-city cop. He doesn't fit here."

The waiter brought Spira's beer. "He thinks there's more behind Stewart's murder than the cube house."

"More?" Hansen said. "What?"

"He didn't say exactly, but he's digging around."

"The Perkinses?"

"That's one idea he mentioned, yeh. He talked about Barbara too. Personal affairs, or maybe some business problem."

"She hasn't got any problems I know," Hansen said.

"And you'd know, wouldn't you?"

"Not necessarily," Hansen denied. "How about Hillock or Bowman? Or Tom McKay. He's back in Fremont."

Spira finished his beer. "Perkins had his office broken

into last night. So did Tucker. You know anything about it?"

"No. Do you?"

"You're sure there's nothing you can tell me, Phil?"

"Not a thing," Hansen said. "How about you? Anything I can help you with?"

They both watched the ocean and each other as Hansen waited for the check.

*

An assistant prosecutor met Beckett at Gordon Stewart's office with the warrant. The assistant wasn't pleased at being a messenger boy. Beckett ignored him, handed the warrant to Judy Muldahr.

"You'll have to break the files open," she said. "I don't have keys to them."

"Do you have a screwdriver?"

She found one in Stewart's desk. The cabinet locks broke easily. Beckett found the Perkins file at the front of the drawer of current cases. The memo was the first document he saw. A short memo, typed, and dated the day Stewart died.

"You ever see this before?"

Judy Muldahr read it. "No. He must have typed it after I left that night. I told you I don't have keys to the files. I could never go to them when he wasn't here."

Beckett examined the lock he had broken. It was a cheap lock on an old cabinet and covered with scratches. He went through the rest of the Perkins file, and the few other files in the current-cases drawer. He found nothing that seemed to be important.

On his way out he studied the lock on the outside door. It was a better and newer lock. It had not been forced.

12

Beckett walked into John Perkins's hospital room.

"I got a warrant to search Stewart's files. I found this. The secretary doesn't have a key."

In the bed, John Perkins read the memo aloud, "*The Perkinses are hiding something, meeting secretly with some stranger. I think they have a scheme to profit from the conflict over their house, and I'll have to resign from the case.*"

Perkins turned the paper in his good hand. "You found this in Stewart's files?"

Beckett nodded. "It means you've been lying. It means you'd have been sure to lose your case if you were exposed. No judge or jury would rule against the other Mar Vista homeowners to let you make a profit out of it."

"A motive for murder," Perkins said. "Except it's not true."

"You're saying it was planted in that file?"

"Do you *type* memos to yourself?"

"Not usually," Beckett said. "The file cabinet could have been picked, but no one forced the outer office door."

"Then you better talk to that secretary."

"Why would she want to plant that memo?"

"Maybe she has a friend," Perkins said. "That Bill Mackay paid me a visit just now. He suggested we sell, move away. If we didn't, we might be in the same danger as Stewart."

"You think he killed Stewart?"

"I think he was threatening us. I think he broke into my office and shot me. I think he planted that memo."

Beckett thought for a time. "I might agree with you, except for that about meeting with some stranger. That has the ring of truth, Perkins."

"I know nothing about any stranger."

"Maybe your wife does."

"I don't like that implication, Beckett!"

"Neither do I," Beckett said. "But it's something that can be checked. The only thing in the memo. Why risk putting it in, maybe ruining the whole trick, when other lies would do?"

"I trust my wife," Perkins said.

"Then you've got nothing to worry about," Beckett said.

*

The Buena Costa County Sheriff's Office is on the first floor of the jail wing of the old courthouse. Sheriff Hoag's private office is at the rear. A large room looking out on a small inner courtyard of green plants and a fountain. Hoag sat behind his desk facing Senator Jesse Eller.

"You think Mackay could have killed Stewart?" Hoag's bland face seemed surprised. Not so much because Bill Mackay could be a killer, but because Eller had said so. "Your own man?"

"I don't know, John," Eller said. He was restless in the leather armchair. "He's capable of it. In spades. For public or private reasons. Either or both."

96

"The break-ins, Jesse? Shooting Perkins?"

"Those too," Eller said. "I once sent him to escort my treasurer to the bank. He had a gas-operated pellet gun. When they stopped later for a beer, Mackay happened to mention that the gas gun tended to build up pressure and go off accidentally. My treasurer was alarmed, told Mackay to do something about it. Bill walked out into the street, it was night—and shot out a street light!"

"You're kidding!"

Eller shook his head grimly. "Another time I happened to say I wished someone would get rid of a certain party for me. The next thing I heard another of my aides came running in and told me Bill had a gun and was on his way to take care of the man! I managed to head him off, don't know if he would really have shot the man, but he complained that I ought to be more accurate in what I said! When he got an order like that, he took care of it."

Hoag frowned. "He's licensed to carry a gun?"

"Yes," Eller said. "Of course, a gun wasn't used."

"No," Hoag said, "and wouldn't it have been dumb to kill Stewart and then let everyone know he was there? A lot smarter to say nothing."

"In a way that's just what worries me," Eller said. "Bill's damned unpredictable. He's so full of bravado he might *want* to be suspected—for the thrill of it and to scare people. I was wrong to send him down here alone. He's tough and loyal, but his judgment can be crazy. A fine assistant, but too damned wild to be allowed to run things. He's useful, will do anything if it's for the 'good' cause, but he can be a walking time bomb."

"Then we better watch him," Hoag said.

"Yes," Eller said, chewed at his fingers, "if it isn't already too late."

*

George Spira leaned over the rail of the *Paloma*.

"Hello, Tom."

Tom McKay, dangling over the outboard side of the sloop in a bosun's chair chipping at paint, smiled up.

"A long time, George."

Spira looked up and down the length of the beautiful but weatherworn sloop as if seeing all the places it had been over the last years.

"How long was it?" he said. "Four years? Five?"

"Five years, seventeen thousand miles," McKay said. "You ought to try it."

"I just might like that."

"What good is all the money if you have to go on working all day and all night for all your life just to make it?"

"Money's never much unless you don't have it," Spira said. "How about that, Tom? You need more money to go off again?"

McKay hauled himself up above the rail, swung inboard, lowered to the deck, and stood up. "You too?"

"Me too what?"

"I killed Stewart to get Barbara's money by remarrying her?"

"It could beat working for it," Spira said.

"It sure as hell would," McKay said, "but I never cared much for killing anything, and I wouldn't like prison."

"Who would, but you never know when it might suddenly seem like the only way to someone," Spira said thoughtfully, almost talking to himself. "Have you seen Barbara?"

"Once."

"She mention any problems? Business or personal? Was she worried about anything?"

"Are you working for the police now, George?"

Spira looked out toward the open sea beyond the distant

breakwater that protected the marina.

"I'm involved in all this," he said. "Maybe I'd just like to know who I'm involved with. Who and what."

"She said nothing to me about trouble or problems."

"Nothing?" Spira said. "Not about the cube house? About what it meant to her and Hansen, maybe? Some complications? About Stewart handling the case and maybe she didn't want him to handle it? About settling for a compromise? Maybe trying to quiet the whole thing down?"

"Why would she talk about all that to me?" McKay said. "I stopped being part of her life twenty years ago."

"Then why did she come to see you?"

"Who knows? Call it a welcome home."

"A kind of reunion?" Spira said. "How often did she do that? Over the twenty years."

McKay began to coil the line still attached to the bosun's chair. "Not very often."

"But she didn't seem to have any special reason to come to you at all, right?"

McKay shrugged. He unhooked the bosun's chair and stowed it away in a deck locker. George Spira leaned against the rail in the sun and watched McKay work.

"Why would Stewart sleep in that room over the garage, Tom?" Spira said after a time.

McKay looked up. "How the hell would I know?"

"You were married to her too."

"That was a long time ago," McKay said. "And I wasn't married to Stewart, was I?"

He finished coiling the line and carried it forward into the bow of the sloop. Spira watched him.

*

The young man patted Cathy Perkins's hand in the cube house.

"I'll be gone a day or so to check out Colonel Hillock,"

he said. "Then maybe I'll dig into Spira some more."

"What about Mackay?" Cathy said. "I just know he's going to do something to us."

"I hope he tries," the young man said. "Maybe you could get him and your husband together, and I could hide and—"

"No!" Cathy cried.

"Okay, okay. I'll just keep a close eye on him when I get back. Don't get nervous, we're doing beautifully. We've even got the good Senator down here now. Just beautiful!"

When his car engine had faded away outside, Cathy gathered up the blueprints and documents strewn around the living room. The ring of the doorbell made her jump like a startled animal. She quickly checked the living room before opening the door. Estelle Bowman smiled over a large bouquet of chrysanthemums.

"I . . . I saw your car," the older woman stammered. "So . . . Here, I want you to have these. I always have nice mums."

"Thank you." Cathy took the flowers. "Won't you come in? Perhaps some coffee?"

"Well, for a moment, but no coffee, dear. It always keeps me awake." Estelle Bowman looked into the sunken living room. "Why, it's quite nice inside, isn't it? Of course, with children a more normal house is—"

"We have no children, Mrs. Bowman," Cathy said.

Estelle Bowman smiled. "But soon, my dear, I'm sure—"

"Children," Cathy said, an edge to her voice, "are a terrible cash and time drain. We're busy enough with our careers, our plans, our social life, the house. Our own lives."

"But," Estelle Bowman fluttered uneasily, "isn't life for people, dear? Where will we get the people? I mean, a

100

house needs people to live in it, doesn't it?"

"We don't seem to think alike," Cathy said, annoyed.

"Think?" Estelle Bowman thought. "Well, I do hope you enjoy the mums. You must plant some. To fill in between the summer annuals and the calendula and Iceland poppies."

"I expect we'll mostly use shrubs," Cathy said. "If any of you leave us a house to plant them around."

Her voice had become bitter, challenging. Estelle Bowman didn't notice. She beamed at Cathy Perkins.

"I know! I'll give you some cuttings. It's time I cut my mums back for second blooming. Yes, I'll go and do that at once."

Nodding to herself, happy, the older woman hurried from the cube house. Cathy Perkins stood motionless for a time, then turned to look at her rich, beautiful, sunken living room.

13

Lee Beckett waited in his car until George Spira drove out of the marina parking lot and turned on the harbor drive toward downtown.

He met Tom McKay climbing ashore from the *Paloma*.

"You know George Spira pretty well?" he asked.

"Fremont's a small place," McKay said.

"What did he want?"

"I'm not sure," McKay said. "Walk me over to the coffee shop. I worked through lunch."

A sea wind was rising in the warm October afternoon, bringing the first signals of evening as they walked along the docks and on toward the rows of shops at the beginning of the breakwater.

"Mostly," McKay said, "he seemed to want about the same as you, a lot of questions. Is he working with you?"

"Not with me," Beckett said. "What questions?"

"About Barbara. Had she wanted Stewart to quit the Perkins case, or at least settle it fast? Was she worried about business problems or complications? The same as you."

"Did he get the same answers?"

"Barbara didn't talk to me about any problems, business or otherwise," McKay said. "Do I gather she's a major suspect?"

"What do you think about it?"

"I'm trying not to think about it at all," McKay said.

They reached the Lobster Pot coffee shop. Beckett went in with McKay. He hadn't eaten any lunch either. Closest to the breakwater in the row of shops that served the Marina, the coffee shop gave a wide view of the sea and the distant islands. They took a window table and both ordered abalone.

"Why does Mrs. Stewart work at all?" Beckett said as they each had a beer while they waited. "Stewart must have made good money, they had no young children and didn't seem to live very high. That old house must be free and clear."

"Barbara always worked. At one thing or another. She insisted. Our first argument after the boy was born."

"Just work? It didn't matter what? A hobby?"

"I'd call it a need," McKay said. "She could never sit at home, hated being just a 'thing.' And it did matter what." McKay took a long drink of his beer, watched the broad expanse of ocean outside the harbor. "It always had to be a *real* job, and for all the money she could get. Nothing volunteer, charitable, or cultural. Her father always said you do what people will pay for. He was the type who thought that any work that didn't make a profit was subversive. I never got along with him. He would have hated Stewart's public defender ideas."

"He's the one who left her the money?"

"When he died a few years ago. Funny, he didn't think women could handle money, left the mother all tied up in a trust where she can only get the income. But he gave Barbara her money straight out. Of course, she gets the trust fund too someday.''

"It would be important to her to make a success of anything she did? And money?"

"Money is how we measure success," McKay said. "Satisfaction is nice, but money is the medal. The bank account, the income. That's what I turned against, chose satisfaction, and that makes me an oddball, right?"

Beckett said nothing. The waiter brought their abalone. The two men began to eat.

*

In the hospital bed John Perkins sat up against the pillows, his left arm strapped across his chest. Cathy smiled at him from the chair across the room under the TV set.

"She really meant to be nice, you know?" Cathy said. "The mums and all. But they just can't really believe we're real."

The shades drawn against the late afternoon sun, it was dim in the antiseptic room. Perkins watched his fellow patient in the other bed, a thin old man putting on his robe and getting up for his daily walk.

"Not quite human," Perkins said. "A common failing, Cath. The 'others' aren't really people. It explains everything from slavery to 'disgusting' foreign foods."

"And weird creatures who don't want children and live in a nightmare house," Cathy said. "Dangerous! Burn them at the stake!"

The thin old man stared at her as he walked slowly to the door. Cathy glared back at him, and Perkins realized that she had changed in the last weeks, her face longer and thinner, almost gaunt. No longer a soft face.

"Sometimes," she said, "I wish we'd never built it, never even thought of our own house."

Perkins watched the old man shuffle out. The door closed.

104

"Cath?" Perkins said. "That prosecutor's investigator Lee Beckett came to see me. He found a memo in Stewart's file on our case. It was a note to himself that he was going to quit our case because we had a plan to profit from the conflict over our house."

"But that's not true, John! You know that. He talked to us, remember, and he wasn't going to quit!"

"Perhaps he wrote the memo later that night," Perkins said, "because this time there was something more. The memo said we were meeting secretly with some stranger. Where would anyone get such an idea? That we were meeting a stranger?"

"How would I know, John?"

"I don't know," Perkins said. He shifted on the bed, pain stabbing across his face. "You've been different lately, almost as if you were sure we would lose the case. Lose everything."

"I'm afraid we will lose the case," Cathy said. She got up and walked around the silent room. "If we do we'll have nothing. Nothing! No home, a useless lot no one else will want, our savings gone, no one who'll want to hire you."

"I asked you earlier if you wanted to pull out."

Cathy paced, said nothing.

"You wanted to go on," Perkins said.

He watched her, but she went on pacing the dim room.

"Beckett thinks that memo might be a fake," Perkins said after a time. "It's typed, unsigned, and could have been put in the file by someone who wants to cast suspicion on us for Stewart's murder, or at least discredit us. Except he thinks that the reference to a 'stranger' has the ring of truth. It can be checked, it's a fact, and would be an unnecessary risk to put in if it wasn't true."

Cathy stopped at the window, looking at the drawn shade as if she could see out through it.

"Don't you trust me, John?"

105

"Trust you? What does that mean, Cath? Trust? I trust you not to have a lover. I trust you not to do anything that would hurt me, or us, intentionally."

She turned and smiled. She walked to the bed.

"Then there you are. That memo means nothing, just some clumsy lie." She bent and kissed him. "I better go. The more you rest, the sooner you'll be out of here."

Perkins said, "I also trust you to always try to help us, protect us. Especially if you're afraid we might lose."

"I'll come back tonight if I can," Cathy said, turned to go. "I might have to work, though."

"Are you in any trouble, Cath?" Perkins said.

"Don't be silly."

She smiled at him, blew a kiss from the door, and went out. Perkins shifted on the bed, and closed his eyes.

*

Barbara Stewart sat out under the twisted old live oak that must have stood there long before the big white house had been built. Before the Yankees had come to Buena Costa County, perhaps even before the Spaniards.

"It was always my favorite tree," she said. The copy of the memo rested on the lap of her loose green dress in the early evening sun filtering through the trees.

"Your husband never mentioned that memo?" Beckett asked.

She glanced down at her lap. "No. Or, rather, I don't know, perhaps he did. Sometimes I didn't listen very closely when he spoke of his work. My fault." She read the memo again. "It's dated that Wednesday, though. He probably wrote it just before he came home and—"

She didn't go on, but leaned her head back against the garden chair to look up through the small leaves and twisted branches of the oak. She seemed to have forgotten the memo.

"You think it's a memo he wrote to himself?" Beckett said.

"If you found it in his files, it must be."

"You realize it could give the Perkinses a motive. They'd look bad if Stewart quit the case, probably lose the house, and maybe something else more important."

She looked around her overgrown yard. "I'm not much of a gardener, am I? No enthusiasm for decorating my little corner." She looked back at Beckett. "I suppose it is a motive of sorts."

"Unless it was planted in his files. By someone out to make them look suspicious. Most men don't type memos."

"No," she said, "but Gordon did. His handwriting was very poor, so he typed everything. A controlled man, not like me."

Beckett got up. "Sheriff Hoag says you never went to identify the body. Your son did."

"I decided there was no point to it, and that I didn't want to see him. Is that so awful, Mr. Beckett?"

"No," Beckett said. "You can claim the body any time now for the funeral."

"William will do that for me too," she said. "There won't be a funeral. Neither Gordon nor I believed in them. William will bury him; I want to keep a different memory."

"Sometimes a funeral helps," Beckett said.

"I'm sure it does," she said. "For many people."

Beckett left her there alone under the old oak, her long face as impassive as a wooden statue under her heavy tan.

He drove north out of Cuyama Beach as the sun went down to the west. He thought about Barbara Stewart and her relation to her husband as he drove.

*

When Cathy Perkins turned into the parking lot of the Fig Tree Motel in downtown Fremont it was already dark. She

107

got out of her car and hurried past the motel office to the last unit in the first row. There was no light at the windows.

She knocked. And knocked again.

There was no sound in the room, and the door was locked.

Cathy hurried back to the motel office.

"Mr. Tarcher," she said to the clerk, "in unit seven. Do you know where he is?"

"Out of town, be back tomorrow." The clerk eyed her up and down. "If you wanted me, I'd be back today."

"Did he leave anywhere he could be reached?"

"Nope, but I'll give you my number?"

"I'd like to leave a message. You have some paper and an envelope?"

"On the writing desk over there."

Cathy wrote a quick message, sealed the envelope, gave it to the clerk, and watched him place it in the slot for unit seven. Then she walked out.

*

George Spira sat in his car in the night. He saw Cathy Perkins leave the motel office. He waited until she had returned to her car and driven away. Then he went into the office.

"That woman who was just here, who did she want?"

The clerk shrugged. "Sorry, I can't—"

"You look thirsty," Spira said, laid a twenty on the desk counter.

The clerk picked up the twenty, folded it neatly lengthwise, fanned the air with it.

"Mr. Burt Tarcher, unit seven. He's out of town."

Spira returned to his car.

14

In the dark of her small bedroom, Judy Muldahr felt his hands on her. On her breasts, big and hard. On her belly. On her thighs. Searching.

He seemed to fill the room, a great, bruising weight that blocked out the light of the moon through the single window, smothering the sound of the surf. Like the surf itself surging up the beach, thrusting under the small house raised on rigid piles buried deep into the sand. Again and again, as endless as the sea itself, as full as the sea and as deep as the sand. Surging and flowing and slowly returning at last to the soft silence of the deep.

Judy lay on the pale bed with her eyes shut. The sound of the surf gentle now, whispering through the dark room.

"Your wife will wonder where you are," she said.

"No she won't," Bill Mackay said. "I don't let her wonder where I am."

"Never?"

"I come home when I come home," he said in the darkness. "Wherever I am, whenever I want, however long."

"And she likes that?"

"She's my wife, she likes it."

Judy touched his naked chest, moved her small hands slowly down his belly to the thick muscles of his thighs. "I guess she's lucky. Where do you get all that drive, power?"

"Practice," Mackay said.

"You almost break a girl in pieces."

"Bend or break, that's being a woman. You don't break."

"But you try, don't you. Try to break me, Bill."

Mackay sat up, swung his bare legs off the bed, and walked to the single window of the small, dark room. Naked in the moonlight, he seemed to stare out at the sea as if he were part of those silent depths.

"A man's power isn't in his sex," he said as if talking not to her but to the night, to the vast sea. "It's not even in his muscles. It's in his mind and in his will. The *will* makes a man."

"Show me."

When he turned from the window he was smiling, and he went to her again. On the bed and moving like the night itself covering her and engulfing.

She breathed slowly beside him. "I hated your mother and Mr. Stewart for making you leave town. We could have been good, Bill."

"They didn't make me leave. No one makes me do anything."

"No one?"

"No one!" He stroked her belly, hard and rough. "I left town because I wanted more than here. I'll get it, too."

"I guess you will," Judy said. She moved her body under his hands. "Bill? That Beckett found a memo in the Perkins file. It said the same as you told me to tell Beckett, that Mr. Stewart was going to quit the Perkins case."

"I told you it was no lie."

110

"I never saw that memo before."

"So he must have typed it to himself that last night."

"You think so?" She watched his dim face on the bed beside her. "He didn't usually type private memos."

"Probably wanted it part of the official file."

"Then you think the Perkinses killed him? Because he was going to quit and expose something they were doing?"

"It's a better motive than any other I've heard."

"Will the police arrest them?"

"It looks like they should, doesn't it?"

"They'd be sure to lose their house then," she said.

"Probably," Mackay said. He sat up in the dark. "I'll call you tomorrow."

"Not yet," she said.

He looked down at her pale shape in the dark room.

"Three for luck," she said.

Mackay smiled, turned to her again.

Someone knocked on the front door of the beach house.

"Company?" Mackay said.

"No one I was expecting."

"See."

She got up, slipped on a robe, and went out into the other rooms. Mackay heard the door open. He heard low voices in the living room. Then a silence seemed to hover over the house. Frowning, Mackay sat up in the bed. Judy appeared in the bedroom doorway. His mother stood beside her.

"A man named Beckett came to me with a private memorandum from Gordon's files," Barbara said. "It was typed, and Gordon would never have typed a private note to himself."

"Did you tell that to Beckett?" Mackay said.

"No, I lied. I knew when I saw it who had to have put it in Gordon's files, and why, and where I would find you."

"You're so sure?"

"You're here, aren't you?" Barbara said.

"And so you had to come around?" Mackay's eyes shined in the dark. "Why? You want to watch? Get some kicks? Okay, come on back to bed, Judy. Momma wants to watch."

"Put some clothes on, you pig," Barbara snapped. She went out into the living room. "Nothing he could do would surprise me, Judy, but I'd have thought you could do better than this."

"The way you did, Mrs. Stewart?" the girl said.

"So?" Barbara sat down in the living room as Judy turned on a lamp. "I'm a lot older and a lot tireder. My choices are more limited. You have too much to offer to settle for this. Phil Hansen isn't much improvement on William, I admit, but he is a little less of an animal."

"I like animals," Judy said. "I always liked Bill."

"Yes." Barbara nodded, sighed. "I wonder if men nauseate themselves too?"

Mackay came from the bedroom with his pants on, tucking in his shirt. His muscles moved in the dim light of the single lamp. His sharp eyes were angry.

"All right, you're here. What do you want, besides discovering us in our disgusting wallowing?"

"You put that memorandum into Gordon's files to make it seem that the Perkinses murdered Gordon."

"I put nothing in Gordon's files."

"That's why you didn't report his death, came to find me."

"Love nests run in our family."

"You'll do anything to gain your ends, won't you? Use anything and anyone."

"You going to report me to the police?" Mackay said.

Barbara watched him. "Do you care who you destroy?"

Mackay began to pace, his shadow giant on the walls of

the small room. "They're guilty! They're criminals, the enemy! I know what they are and what they want. They want to destroy *us*, the community! All I have to do is prove it, expose them!"

"You mean you know they're guilty of something you consider criminal, and you're going to convict them of something no matter what it is or if they did it."

"I'm going to stop them, I don't care how. We have to stop them, and Tucker, and all the subversive damned weaklings!"

"No lie is too low?"

"It's not a lie! They're dangerous."

Barbara stood up. "Gordon's death was very convenient."

"I'll use any weapon I can find," Mackay said.

Barbara went to the door. "Your wife has a special dinner waiting for you. She's a fool."

*

Beckett saw her at the corner table in the quiet cocktail lounge, muted music playing softly for the couples holding hands in the flickering candlelight. She was alone. He sat down.

"Your son didn't know where Hansen was, said I'd find you here," Beckett said.

"You found me," Ann Hansen said.

The short, blond woman waved to the waitress. Her lined face seemed softer in the shadowy lounge, the remains of a youthful prettiness. Thicker now, worn, the quiet drinking brought back a vague illusion of a once slim girl. She ordered Scotch. Beckett ordered a beer. He showed her the memo.

"Have you ever seen this? We found it in Gordon Stewart's files. It could be a fake, planted there."

She glanced at the memo. "No."

113

"We can check the typewriter."

"Check. I don't have a typewriter."

"Your husband does. In his office."

She drank, put down her glass, picked up the memo. She read it through. Carefully. She put it down. Drank.

"Why would Phil care if Stewart had been going to quit the Perkins case or not? He sold them the lot, that's all. There's no more in it for us, one way or the other. Talk to George Spira about Mar Vista, not Phil."

"He seems to care about the cube house," Beckett said. "Why?"

"I don't know. Public relations? Community spirit? He never did have what it takes to be tough in business."

"Does he have any complications in his business?"

"No!"

"Any changes in his business lately?"

"No!"

"Maybe Barbara Stewart has some problems in business?"

She drank. "What the hell do you want, Beckett? What are you trying to do, find a motive for Phil to kill Stewart?"

"Would you tell me if he had killed Stewart?"

"If he killed Stewart, I'd kill *him!* With my own hands! If he did that to me, to us!" She drank, drank again. "I had everything as a child. My father knew how to make money, and I was the princess. Whatever I wanted. I quit four colleges, he still sent me to a fifth to graduate. I was good in school. I had fun back then. I had any boy I wanted. I was alive."

She signaled to the waitress for another whisky. "You ever been to Barbados? We went there for a month. Warm sea, skin diving, sailing, outlying little islands with big old hotels and food you can't imagine. Sun all day, fun all night. I loved Barbados, it was living."

114

The waitress set down her Scotch. "That was twenty years ago with another man. I didn't marry him. The high point of my life. I've wanted to go back ever since, and I will!"

"Who doesn't want to go to Barbados," Beckett said.

"I don't care what other people want. I did once, I cared about other people, but I don't anymore."

"You care about your own future. You'd kill Hansen if he destroyed your future by killing Stewart. Would you kill someone else to defend your future? To protect Hansen's future?"

She thought. "I don't know. Perhaps I would." She drank. "He's all I have for a future. That's how it works."

"But you didn't."

"No, I didn't."

Beckett paid for his beer.

*

Bill Mackay drove north from the beach, through Fremont dark and deserted at past ten o'clock, and stopped at a gaudy roadhouse on the highway to San Vicente. Two men leaned against a dusty pickup truck. One was tall and wiry, the other was stocky. They both wore work clothes and western hats. Bill Mackay walked up to them.

"Hey, old buddy," the tall one said.

"You clowns look as mean as ever." Mackay grinned.

"Too long, Billy boy," the stocky one said.

"You got something good?" the tall one asked.

"Could be," Mackay said. "Come on inside."

They went into the tavern, a wave of violent music sweeping out into the night as they opened the door.

In the parking lot a man got out of a Ford Pinto. He went to the telephone booth at the gas station next door.

"Mr. Spira? He just met two guys at the Red Roan Tavern. They've got a pickup with a California license, but

115

they look from out of town. Yessir. Okay."

The man went back to the Pinto, got in, and sat smoking.

*

There was light in Prosecutor Tucker's window high in the darkened courthouse in San Vicente. Beckett went up, closed the door behind him, and sat rubbing his eyes.

"Long day?" Tucker said. "Any progress?"

"Not much." Beckett leaned back, stretched out his legs. "That Barbara Stewart is a strange woman. I can't pin her down, but there's something wrong, something on her mind."

"Not just Stewart's death?"

Beckett shook his head. "There's more, I know it. They're all jumpy as if waiting for an explosion. George Spira is going around talking to everyone, and that Tom McKay is hiding something. I'd swear on that."

"What about Perkins? How is he?"

"Sitting up, but worried." Beckett tossed the memo to Tucker. "I found that in Gordon Stewart's file on the Perkinses. It gives them a motive, even though I still don't think the cube house alone is enough for murder. Maybe what Stewart implies they're involved in *is* enough. If the memo isn't a fake."

"Planted in the file to frame them?"

"Perkins says by Bill Mackay," Beckett said. "A faked memo is his style, but why in hell would he kill Stewart?"

"Maybe that's what we don't know yet," Tucker said.

Beckett nodded. He had the small brass disk in his hand. He studied it moodily.

"Hoag isn't doing any better," Tucker said, "and the newspapers are killing me with innuendo."

116

"I should work on my other cases," Beckett said.

"No, stay on this, Lee. Finish it."

Beckett got up. "Then give that memo to Hoag, have him check it out against Stewart's typewriter."

Alone, Charles Tucker watched the silent city outside his windows.

15

George Spira arrived late in his office overlooking the construction yard the next morning. He called in his yard foreman. It was the man who had watched Bill Mackay from the Pinto.

"Well, Pete?"

"They were in the tavern a couple of hours, chief, then the two in the pickup checked into the El Prado Motel near the marina. Mackay went home to the Stewart house in Cuyama Beach."

"That's all?"

"That's it. Mackay was at Judy Muldahr's house on the beach earlier, like I told you last night. That blond mother of his showed up there for maybe ten minutes."

"Okay, Pete, and thanks."

Spira worked for the rest of the morning on paperwork, but his mind wasn't on it. It was only eleven A.M. when he gave up, went to his car, and drove south to Cuyama Beach.

A young woman he didn't know let him in, and took him out to the backyard. Barbara Stewart sat alone under a large old live oak. Her long, tanned face was stiff under her blond hair, and she wore a pale gray tailored suit. As if she were about to go out on business, but not going.

"Brooding's no good, Barbara," Spira said.

"What is good?"

Spira sat facing her. "When's the funeral?"

"No funeral, George. He didn't like funerals. He used to say life is for the living. I wonder if life is for anyone?"

"All we've got, and it goes on."

She smiled. "You're a practical man, aren't you? No abstractions. And you didn't come to ask about a funeral."

"Is there anything going on in your office, Barbara? A big deal, a project, something the cube house thing could be messing up, complicating?"

"No."

"I might be able to help. You or Hansen."

"I don't need any help."

"Do you know what your son is up to?"

"No."

"He's got a couple of rough-looking friends in town. He's already in trouble over not reporting to the police, and maybe over those break-ins."

She watched a scrub jay in the oak. "I don't care what William does."

"You know he's playing with Gordon's secretary."

"Yes, I know. Stupid girl."

"Do you know a man named Burt Tarcher? Did Gordon?"

She shook her head. "No."

"You're sure you're not in some kind of business trouble? At Hansen's office?"

She didn't answer, continued to look up at the raucous jay in the twisted branches of the old oak. Spira stood up.

"Take it easy, Barbara, okay?"

119

"Easy?" she said, watched the bright bird. "Yes, I'll take it easy."

Spira walked back through the big house. He looked back once, saw her still sitting there under the tree as if she never planned to move again.

In his car he drove up Beacon Road. At the first narrow cross lane he turned in, parked facing out toward Beacon Road, and shut off his motor.

*

Beckett was eating his breakfast when the telephone rang.

"Sorry," Tucker said from the other end, "I've got to change my orders. You're needed in court in an hour to testify in the Bailey rape trial."

He had to wait two hours to give his few minutes of testimony, and then Sheriff Hoag insisted on giving him the report on the memo and typewriter in person. The memo *had* been typed on Stewart's office machine, so real or fake was still open.

"If it is fake," Beckett said, "it just about has to be Bill Mackay who planted it."

"Or the secretary," Hoag said. "But I think it's real. I never trusted those Perkinses."

"Not solid people like Bill Mackay," Beckett said.

He went up to his own office to send a cablegram to the police in Papeete, and it was past noon when he drove again along Beacon Road toward the Stewart house. A Nova passed him going toward Fremont. Barbara Stewart was at the wheel. She didn't seem to see Beckett, stared straight ahead as she drove.

He was thinking about her driving the Nova instead of her Cadillac that had killed Stewart, and only barely noticed the second car that came fast behind her. A big Ford, and George Spira was driving. Spira didn't see Beckett either,

120

his eyes intent on the Nova ahead of him. Spira was following Barbara Stewart.

There were children's voices and laughter in the big white house when Beckett pulled up to the front door. A young woman answered his ring.

"Mrs. Mackay? Is your husband home?"

"He's eating his breakfast. He doesn't like—"

Mackay's voice called, "Back here, Beckett."

Beckett went in and back to the large kitchen. Mackay sat in a breakfast nook overlooking the broad rear yard. Bare-chested in pajama bottoms, he was eating eggs. He nodded toward an old enamelware coffeepot on the stove.

"Help yourself. That's the only way to make coffee."

Beckett poured himself a cup of coffee, sat across from Mackay in the booth. Through the wide old windows the trees and brush of the backyard were pleasant and peaceful in the October noon sunlight.

"You heard about the memo I found?" Beckett said.

"Yeh. You arrested the Perkinses yet?"

"Not yet," Beckett said. "How did Stewart find out about the Perkinses planning to profit from the melee over their house? And about secret meetings with some stranger?"

"Don't know where he dug up the facts on the scheme, whatever it is, but I told him about that stranger. Maybe Gordon found him, got his story."

"Then you seem to be the only one who knew about this secret stranger," Beckett said.

"And Gordon," Mackay said, took a mouthful of eggs.

"Yes, and Stewart."

Mackay chewed toast. "Maybe if you and Hoag had been doing your jobs right you'd have spotted him by now. I found out on my own, saw the guy and that Cathy Perkins, before anything had happened to Gordon. She's met him other times since, and he's been nosing around all over town.''

"Can you describe him? You know his name?"

"He's young, kind of jazzy, wears crazy casual clothes like a college kid, and makes a lot of phone calls. He's staying at the Fig Tree Motel, and his name's Burt Tarcher.''

"You've been busy.''

"Call it detective work.''

"All part of your job for Senator Eller? Or for Maxwell Bowman?''

"Call it community service. I care.''

Beckett finished his coffee. Mackay got up and poured another cup for himself, refilled Beckett's cup.

"Your father—'' Beckett began.

"Stepfather.''

"Your father,'' Beckett said, "Tom McKay. Does he need money? To keep that boat, maybe? For another cruise?''

"Money?'' Mackay seemed puzzled. Then he laughed. "You mean Barbara's money? Hell, no way he could get—''

"By remarrying, maybe?''

"Re . . . ! You mean get rid of Gordon so . . . ? For her money? Tom McKay! Christ, Beckett, he'd never do that. It's not in the old dropout. He's a runaway, hide in the sand. He wasn't even man enough to keep a woman or run a family. He can't act, take control. All he can do is run from reality.''

"You think he failed you? Twenty years ago?''

"Didn't he? He should have slapped her down, kept us.''

"And you've been acting the man he wasn't ever since,'' Beckett said. "Man enough to kill, for money or anything else?''

122

Mackay sipped at his coffee, watched a tawny cat stalking a loud, angry scrub jay out under the trees.

"If I needed money that much, or anything else, you can bet on it." Mackay got up. "I've got business."

He walked out of the kitchen. Beckett sat finishing his coffee alone, watched the angry cat outside as the jay flew up into an oak and mocked it.

*

You reached the restaurant through a long arched arcade lined with shops, and across a sheltered patio-court where the Fremont businessmen and the ladies out shopping ate lunch at tables in the warm sun. It had only a number, the restaurant, 1149, and Barbara Stewart had taken a corner table for herself and Ann Hansen.

"Guilty-conscience lunch, Barbara?" Ann Hansen said.

"I'm not sure. Do you really care about it?"

Ann Hansen ate her frittata and thought. Barbara Stewart watched her closely. The two women were in violent contrast. Barbara Stewart tall and angular, her high-boned face darkly tanned, cool and trim in her tailored suit, looking younger than her forty-five years. Ann Hansen shorter, thicker, her heavy face pale and her loose brown dress careless and sloppy. A woman who didn't care that she looked older than she was. Opposites, yet alike, a sense of relation.

"I care about what he does," Ann Hansen said at last. "Why do you want him, Barbara?"

"I don't know that I do," Barbara said. She toyed with her crepes. "He wanted me. That's what it is, isn't it? They want the sex, the use of our bodies. They collect our bodies, and feel strong, and we like that. It flatters us, makes us feel triumphant over other women. They'll share us, but we compete over them."

"You think we should share him?" Ann said, eating.

"I didn't—"

"But I know what you mean, what we want," Ann said, nodding as she ate. "It feels good to watch them while they take you. They're so damned eager, so intense. They need so much."

"And we need that need," Barbara said. "Is that really what it is? The need to be used?"

"Maybe," Ann said, sat back. "I don't know really, not anymore."

The waiter brought tea. Barbara poured.

"I suppose I did want him," she said. "He was there in the office, we were together, and he had a wife. He had a woman, and he still wanted me, and that flattered me."

"Why not?" Ann said. "I don't care about that now, but I care about his time, you know? He's not going to shirk his work to play with you. I won't let you tie him up."

"His work? You care about that? The money?"

"That's what I care about, and now that you're free, you better walk away. Men can get wild ideas. You had your fling, and now it better stop. Clear?"

"Yes," Barbara said, slowly. "He has an importance to you, and now that I'm free I don't really want him."

"So we can finish our lunch," Ann said.

They both laughed. It was laughter without much humor, and it stopped as the short man sat down at their table.

*

In his green corduroy jeans and short jacket, a heavy gold medallion at his bare throat, Burt Tarcher walked into the Brass Kettle in downtown Fremont. He saw Cathy Perkins through the last of the lunch crowd, alone at a rear table.

"I got your message, what's up?"

"John knows," Cathy said. "They all know!"

"Whoa!" Tarcher said, sat down. "What do they know?"

"About you, me, the meetings, everything!"

"Who I am? What we're doing?"

"I . . . I don't know. If they don't yet, they will, and—"

"Okay, okay." Tarcher looked around the room that was emptying now that lunchtime was over. "It's been an advantage nosing around on the sly with you helping, but I've been tailed off and on anyway. So they know, it doesn't matter."

"It could cost us the house! We'll lose!"

"I've got my rights, and so have you. Call it free enterprise, and we're perfectly legit."

"They'll say we planned it from the start! Arranged it all for you! Oh, why did I agree to do it?"

"For a lot of money. Even if you lose, you come out safe," Tarcher said. He leaned forward. "Listen, I've been down to the Army base where Hillock had his last command, and there's a beautiful stink! Seems the good colonel made a private deal before he retired. Not big, just built a pair of houses to sell later for what should have been a modest profit."

Tarcher grinned happily. "Except it turns out that he used enlisted men to build them, and maybe some government materials! Get it? He had the houses largely built by soldiers—for free! Free labor! So when he sold them, after he'd retired, he made a whopping profit. He bought the Mar Vista house with some of the money, banked the rest."

"Is that legal?"

"I don't know, but it'd be hard to prove anyway. The EMs 'volunteered' to help, worked on their 'spare' time—for some cases of beer and probably some 'favors' in return, but it'll look like just a nice, friendly gesture. Some people have been after the services for years about things like that—using enlisted men as servants, baby-sitters, cooks, mechanics for the private benefit of officers. Hillock just took it a step on, and there's a real row down there—behind the scenes, of course, very hush-hush right now."

He laughed, "Only it won't be hush-hush anymore, right? There's no connection to the mess here, but I'll make one—a typical example of the actions of privileged right-wingers like the Mar Vista gang! Maybe worse—a man who cheats like that would do anything for money, or to protect his money, eh?"

"You mean . . . Mr. Stewart?"

"Could be. Hillock's an old soldier, a trained killer, and his wife may be even tougher. My contact down at the base says they think the deal was her idea more than his."

Cathy sat silent, her once-soft face drawn and narrow.

"You don't care if something's true or not, do you?"

"You have to find out what's true, show what could be."

"Mr. Stewart might have known about us, me and you, before he was killed," she said, told him about the memo.

"So what?" Tarcher said lightly.

"How important is all of this to you?"

"Not that important," Tarcher said. "I'm one of the good guys, the poor and downtrodden. We don't kill people."

He grinned at Cathy. Her hands twisted together.

16

In the shadows of the arcade between the street and the sunny courtyard where Barbara Stewart and Ann Hansen were finishing their lunch, George Spira stood watching the two women. He had been there from the start, wondering if it was all about Phil Hansen or something else?

The man who came from the rear parking lot and sat down with the two women was short, had thin brown hair and steel-rimmed glasses, and wore a nondescript cheap blue suit. Oscar Krankl. Spira couldn't tell which of the women he was talking to, but there was an urgency in the way he leaned, and he glanced around nervously. He stood up, and left as abruptly as he had appeared.

Spira watched the women. Would they follow Krankl? Or one of them?

"That's quite a pair," the voice said behind him.

Bill Mackay stood in the arcade. Spira went on watching the two women. They were ready to leave.

"Comparing notes on Hansen," Mackay said. "Women!"

"Or on business?" Spira said without turning.

"Which one are you interested in, Spira?"

"Both."

Spira watched the women pay their separate checks, and walk together toward the rear parking lot.

"Which one're you tailing?" Mackay said.

Spira turned. "I don't like you, Mackay. I don't like how you think, how you operate, or what you stand for. As far as I'm concerned you're nothing but a big mistake."

"Too bad," Mackay said, "we're on the same side."

"No we're not." Spira pushed past Mackay and strode away along the arcade out into the main street.

Mackay flushed, stood chewing angrily on his mustache. Spira didn't notice. He wasn't thinking about Mackay.

He was thinking about the two women and Oscar Krankl, and when he reached his car parked at the curb he didn't stop but went on across the busy downtown street to the County Recorder's office on the third floor of the courthouse. He went into the office of County Clerk Mel Phillips.

"I want to look at the real estate records, Mel. For the whole last year."

"It'll cost you two bucks an hour now, George."

"Is there somewhere private?"

"Empty office right off the main room."

Spira went out to gather the records. A young man in a green corduroy jean suit was talking to the records clerk.

"Hillock, right. A house in Mar Vista Estates."

"There's a charge of two dollars, Mr. Tarcher."

"Okay, I'll—"

Spira walked up to the young man. "You're the one who's been meeting the Perkinses! Who the hell are you?"

"That's not your business, Mr. Spira," Tarcher said.

"It could damn well be police business!"

"Don't try to intimidate me, Spira."

"How do you know me? What do you want? What kind

128

of game do you have with the Perkinses?''

"I'll be back later," Tarcher said to the clerk, and walked out of the Recorder's office.

Spira stared after him for a time, then got the records he wanted, and closed the door of the empty office behind him.

*

Beckett found Gordon Stewart's office locked, drove on to the small beach house near the harbor. Judy Muldahr opened the door. She wore a bikini that didn't suit her big body. She led him into the small living room that overlooked the city beach and the distant breakwater on the far side of the harbor.

"Not working today?" Beckett said.

"A dead man doesn't need a secretary. I told Mrs. Stewart I was quitting."

"What did she say?"

"Good luck," the girl said. "What do you want, Mr. Beckett?"

Out of the office, in the bikini, she seemed suddenly a different girl. A woman, and the bikini not that bad on her after all, big as she was and with the short black hair. The kind of girl who made Beckett feel old when she called him *Mr.* Beckett. There would be a man, or men, somewhere not too far away, and something else. A hardness. Not quite the proper and devoted secretary he had seen in Stewart's office.

"We checked that memo," he said. "It was typed on your office machine."

"You thought maybe it hadn't been?"

"Perkins thinks it's a fake, planted in the files."

"What else would he say?"

Through the front window Beckett could see across the harbor to the marina. The *Paloma* was easy to spot. There seemed to be people on it. He wished he had a pair of binoculars.

"The memo doesn't say much, but it implies that Stewart knew what the Perkinses were doing. How did he find out?"

She shrugged. "Snooped around, I guess. I mean, he didn't tell me what he did most of the time, you know?"

"But his stepson, Mackay, told him about the stranger?"

"I don't know, maybe. They had a meeting in the office."

"Who else did he meet with those last days?"

"On the Perkins thing?" She frowned. "God, he met with so many, you know? The Perkinses right that night. His wife and George Spira. He could have met anyone at Tucker's rally."

On the *Paloma* across the harbor a man left the boat. A young man, Beckett thought, but it was too far to be sure.

"But Mackay's the only one who's talked about the stranger," he said. "You know Mackay pretty well, Judy?"

"I know him."

"And you like him?"

"I liked him when he lived here before."

"Old friends?" Beckett said. "Does he have a key to Stewart's office?"

"I don't think so."

"No, I wouldn't think he did," Beckett said. "Okay, if you remember anything about the memo, call me."

He left without looking at her again.

*

Judy Muldahr stared at the closed door, heard Beckett drive away. She went to the telephone. At Eller headquarters they called Bill Mackay to the phone.

"Beckett's suspicious about that memo," Judy said.

"He came to you? What did you tell him?"

"What could I tell him? What is there to tell?"

"Nothing," Mackay said. "I'll see you later."

"I'll be here."

In the silent room, the light sound of a low surf outside, Judy sat beside the telephone. She picked up the receiver.

"Mr. Spira, please." She listened. "All right, will you tell him Judy Muldahr called. He can call me."

She hung up, thought, dialed again.

"Mr. Bowman? Judy Muldahr, Gordon Stewart's secretary. Yes. I'd like to talk to you. Yes, it's important. Why don't you come to my house? As soon as you can."

*

Alone in the empty office of the County Recorder, George Spira worked into the evening. He read through the records of all the real estate transactions in the county for the last year, concentrating on the Fremont area. It was late when he finished. He returned the records and left.

He went to an Italian restaurant near the harbor and ate his dinner. He had four beers, frowning into them as he drank.

*

Beckett identified himself in the office of the Fig Tree Motel.

"Mr. Tarcher isn't in," the clerk said.

"Let me into the unit, I'll wait," Beckett said. "Don't tell him."

"Sure, Mr. Beckett."

In the silent motel room Beckett looked slowly around. He saw the typewriter on the desk, the gaudy youthful swinger clothes hanging up, the reference books on Buena Costa County, and the thick file folder. He found no weapons.

With the twilight outside the curtained windows, Beckett sat down to wait.

*

George Spira knocked on the door of the frame bungalow in the area of older houses near the harbor. As he waited in the dusk, Spira looked at the postage stamp front lawn, the shabby neighboring houses, and the large mobile-home cruiser in the driveway. Oscar Krankl opened the door.

"George? What's up?"

"You tell me," Spira said. "In private, Oscar."

Krankl glanced into the house. "It's dinnertime. Make it tomorrow at my—"

"Now," Spira said.

"Hey listen, I don't have to—!"

"I know, Oscar. You understand? The question is what do I do. I want the details, and right now."

Krankl was pale. A thin woman with black hair beginning to go gray came from the dining room. "Oscar? What is it? Your dinner will get cold."

"I'll be busy awhile, Maritha," Krankl said.

Mrs. Krankl watched the two men come into the house and go into a bedroom. They closed the door.

When Spira came out twenty minutes later he was alone, Krankl silent in the dim bedroom behind him. Spira went to the hall telephone, dialed.

"I want to see you. Spira. I'm with Krankl right now, and I want to talk! Okay, I'll be there."

*

Burt Tarcher stopped just inside the motel room door. "You're Beckett."

In an armchair, Beckett held the file folder. "Quite a story. I never knew Buena Costa was such a hotbed of rich exploiters, establishment power."

Tarcher came on into the room. "You better have a warrant! That's confidential data, private property."

Beckett smiled. "It's my county, you wrote about how corrupt we are. Besides, from this story you don't even

132

believe in private property. What magazine is it, Tarcher?''

Tarcher sat on the bed, swung his legs up. *"People's Voice.* The eyes and ears of the 'Now' generation. One million circulation plus every week, and building.''

Beckett nodded. ''Down with the imperialist American establishment. Bill Mackay would call it subversive.''

''Mackay would call *The National Geographic* subversive,'' Tarcher said, stretched his legs. ''We think of ourselves as unaligned, the Third World, against all oppression anywhere.''

''Did you set it all up?'' Beckett said. ''Tell them to put the house in Mar Vista to challenge the covenant, raise hell?''

''I wish I could say yes, it's a great story, but we didn't. Just luck. Not that anyone'll believe that.''

''I believe it. What deal did you make?''

''Twenty thousand down, plus a bundle for every week we keep it running. We get exclusive rights to their whole story, all that happens as it goes along, everything the other side does, daily reports on the trial, what everyone says, inside stuff, opinions, the works.''

''With both Perkinses?''

Tarcher hesitated. ''No, just with her.''

''Those office break-ins were your work?''

''Hell no!'' Tarcher sat up.

''Yeh,'' Beckett said. ''So the Perkinses are the good guys, Mar Vista and the county the baddies. Two little people who wanted their dream house pushed around by the rich, exclusive, and powerful. Violence, even murder, to protect privilege.''

''Something like that,'' Tarcher said.

''When you come out, it won't help them in court.''

''All the better. We—'' Tarcher stopped, uneasy.

''Yeh,'' Beckett said again. ''It wouldn't be good for your

133

story if they won, would it? No propaganda angle to that."

Tarcher was silent, watchful. Beckett got up, walked closer to the bed and the magazine man.

"You want them to lose. The more injustice the better," Beckett said. "Stewart's murder makes big headlines. And his death makes it more likely that they *will* lose."

"Don't try to pin that on me! You can't—!"

Beckett bent down, his face close to Tarcher. "You stupid little jerk, the way you've been messing around I could pin anything I want on you! You could have planted that memo to make sure your deal came out and made the Perkins lose! You're a prime suspect for those break-ins; I could get a warrant on you for that right now! I could add suspicion of murder anytime!"

Beckett was breathing hard, staring into Tarcher's face. The gaudy young man licked his lips. Dry lips.

"What do you want?" Tarcher said.

"Good," Beckett said. He straightened up. "I want everything you've dug up. All of it, or I'll break you open."

Tarcher nodded. He told Beckett about Colonel Hillock and the two houses he had built with army labor. He told him about Bill Mackay and the two strangers he had met, and about Mackay seeing a lot of Judy Muldahr. He told about Cathy Perkins admitting Stewart had mentioned quitting, and about George Spira watching, talking, and looking up real estate records.

"Both the Perkinses could have killed Stewart?"

"I guess so."

"And Spira was checking real estate tonight?"

"Yes. I saw him."

"Okay. How come you haven't run the first story yet?"

"We were going to wait until the trial opened. Better impact that way."

"Now?"

134

"You've got it there. Next week."

"You better hold off. Until we solve the murder."

Tarcher nodded. Beckett dropped the file on the bed as he turned to the door.

*

George Spira's house in Mar Vista was dark and silent. Beckett drove back into Fremont to the construction yard. There was light in Spira's second-floor office, moving shadows.

A broad, stocky older man turned as Beckett walked into Spira's office.

"He's . . . dead."

George Spira sat in his desk chair, his eyes wide and staring, two ragged, black and bloody holes in his chest.

17

Beckett examined the dead man. The body was still warm. A big gun, from close range; Spira's shirt burned and the bullets had gone through leaving two holes the size of fists coming out. There were no marks on the chair or the wall behind the desk, and no blood on the floor or chair.

"Who are you?" he asked the stocky older man.

"Pete Albano, yard foreman. I was working late, and—"

"You heard the shots?"

"No! Not a sound. I saw the light up here. I didn't know Mr. Spira was here. He wasn't earlier, you know? I came up to talk, and . . . and . . ." He stared at the dead man.

"Okay, call the sheriff. Tell him I'm here. Lee Beckett."

While the foreman called, Beckett went out and down to the dark construction yard. He saw the big car parked near an outside flight of stairs that led up to the second floor of the office building. The hood was hot.

The blood was there, all over the floor and the front seat, and the two bullets had ripped the driver's door.

Newspaper covered the floor under the steering wheel,

and a trail of blood led from the car to the outside stairs and up them until it faded at the top. The door at the top was unlocked. Inside, small patches of blood led to Spira's office. Beckett heard the foreman explaining things to Sheriff Hoag.

He found the raincoat on the corridor floor inside the backstairs door. A large man's raincoat, with blood all over the back, no blood inside, and no holes.

He returned to the car, examined the back and front seats again. He found the button on the floor of the passenger's side of the front seat. A bloody button the size of a nickel, with a metal loop to attach it, and strands of gray thread on the loop. The button was covered with a soft gray material.

Beckett put the button into his pocket, and went up to wait for Sheriff Hoag. It was a woman's button.

*

The *Paloma* moved gently in its dock in the night.

Barbara Stewart stood forward looking over the side at the dark slick of the water.

An odor of salt mud in the light October wind.

She walked the length of the boat, her hands rubbing along the rail, and stood at the stern looking down at the water. Tall in the weak light of the single high bulb on the dock, she wore a navy-blue wool dress with a high turtleneck and a slim skirt below her knees above brown sandals.

A car screeched in the parking lot.

There was music somewhere, voices on a boat on the far side of the marina.

"Barbara?"

Tom McKay stood on the pier. He came aboard.

"I'm sorry about Stewart."

She walked toward the bow. "William buried him. Quietly. A quiet man should go quietly. Silent and alone."

137

"Do they know anything yet?"

She sat down on the deck house. "Do you remember Jimmie Fitch?"

"No," McKay said. "You better go home, Barbara."

"You don't remember Jimmie? I remember Jimmie. Does Jimmie remember me? Is that the question?" She smiled up.

"Yes, I remember Fitch. You were going to marry him out of college. It's the past, Barb."

"My father didn't like him," she said. "Was that why?"

"It's cold," McKay said. "Come below."

She stood, walked away from the cabin. "He never liked any of my boys. His daughter hadn't gotten a college degree to pamper some oaf and take out the garbage. The princess, his lady intellectual."

McKay looked around at the silent boats, the distant parking lot, the single far-off boat where the voices were.

"He liked you though, I remember," Barbara said, her hands rubbing at the rail. "A solid man. He was so often wrong, had no idea what you really wanted. From me. From life."

"Barb—"

McKay took her arm. She pulled away, roughly. She glared at McKay, rubbed her arm through the blue wool.

"I was happy with him! He was a wonderful man! He was the best man!"

"He was fine, a good father," McKay said. "You shouldn't be here. Come below now, or go on home. Okay?"

She leaned heavily against the rail. A tall woman. She looked out across the harbor to the lights of the city.

"Home, yes. I have to go home."

She turned and swayed along the lightly moving deck to the gangplank as if she would fall. She laughed aloud.

138

"Wheeeee! It's like a carnival ride! I won't fall, Tom. I never fall. I do have to go home, at least that."

Tom McKay watched her until her tall figure disappeared, the sound of her sandals faded away in the parking lot. He heard her car start. When it had gone, he stood on the boat listening to the night as if he expected to hear some special sound. There was nothing.

*

Beckett leaned against the wall in a corner of George Spira's office. It looked like a small riot. Since it was the city, the Fremont police, behind Detective Captain Daniel Rogvin, were there as well as Sheriff Hoag and his deputies.

"It's got to tie into the Stewart killing," Hoag said, "but I can use your cooperation, Dan."

That didn't seem to please Captain Rogvin. Cooperation had never been Hoag's long suit.

"George had a lot of angles," Rogvin decided. "It could be nothing to do with the Stewart case."

The captain wasn't noted for sharing authority either.

"I doubt that, Dan," Hoag said.

The sheriff smiled. So did Rogvin. They were both good at smiling.

Beckett watched it all from his corner as the horde of police searched the office and the yard outside under garish floodlights. They examined the car, dusted it, vacuumed it, photographed it, and put everything moveable into plastic bags for the laboratory. The assistant coroner made his report.

"Two pills at close range. Some big, hard-hitting gun like an army Colt. Somebody's souvenir, I'll bet. We used to get a lot of them after the war. An hour ago now, give or take half an hour. Obviously not in this office."

They took the body out. The foreman repeated his story for Hoag and Rogvin. He seemed to be lost in that hopeless haze of disbelief an irreversible tragedy can bring.

"He'd been going around talking to the people in that crazy house mess, watchin' some of 'em. Had me tail that Mackay guy for him. I spotted Mackay meet a couple of tough-lookin' characters from somewheres, saw him put some time in at the Muldahr girl's house."

They found the two bullets in the car door. One was in poor shape, the other was good enough for ballistics checking. Rogvin and the Fremont men dug into Spira's business contracts, went off to question his employees. Hoag instructed two of his deputies.

"Get out there and see if you can find out what he was doing, where he was, where it happened. Maybe someone saw or heard something, or maybe the lab can help." Hoag came over to Beckett. "Anything more you can tell me?"

"I think so," Beckett said, and told Hoag about meeting Burt Tarcher. "He confirmed what that foreman said about Mackay and the two cronies and Judy Muldahr. He also said Spira was in the County Recorder's office this afternoon checking some records, and I can tell you Spira was out at the Stewart house around noon, could have been tailing Barbara Stewart. It's somewhere to start tracing him."

"Good," Hoag nodded. "So that's the Perkinses deal? Sell the whole story to that damned subversive rag? Stewart would have dropped the case if he knew that for sure."

"If he knew," Beckett said.

"It's a motive for murder, and maybe Spira dug it up too," Hoag said. "The way I work it out, the killer was sitting in the passenger's seat. They were talking, Spira sitting sideways behind the wheel to face the killer. He got hit close up, the slugs went into the door."

Beckett nodded. "The killer shoved the body over, spread newspaper on the floor and put on the raincoat to keep blood off him, and drove here. He dragged the body up to the office, and took off.''

"Spira's raincoat, the foreman says he always kept it in the car for visiting construction sites," Hoag said. ''What I don't get is why he went to all that trouble to drag the body up to the office. We were sure to spot the car fast.''

"I don't know," Beckett said. "Maybe when we find out why, it'll tell us something. Or maybe we're dealing with someone who never killed before and just wasn't thinking straight, half fell apart. Thought it would confuse us, gain time.''

"I'd say he killed once before, at least.''

"Stewart?''

"It has to be," Hoag said. He sat on the edge of a desk, looked out the high window at the dark night. "I admit we haven't been pushing too hard on Stewart. I figured to myself it was probably suicide or some accident even with the change of cars. But this is real, and I'm going after them all hard. We'll hammer everyone involved now, get this killer!''

"Yeh," Beckett said.

He left Hoag bawling orders to his hard-working deputies, and went down and out to his car. He lit a cigarette, and sat in the car thinking. He became aware of the other car. An orange Nova parked across the dark industrial street. Besides the last three sheriff's cars, it was the only car on the street, and there was someone in it.

Beckett opened his car door.

The other car started and drove past him with its lights still out before he could even yell.

*

In his rearview mirror, Bill Mackay saw Beckett out in the road staring after him. Mackay smiled, but it was a thin smile, his face tense and violent under the black mustache.

141

He drove through Fremont to the highway that led to Mar Vista Estates. The cube house stood dark above the access road. There were no cars parked at the silent house.

Mackay drove back into Fremont to St. Stephen's Hospital, and went up to the third floor without stopping at the desk or announcing his visit. John Perkins looked up from the sketchboard he was working on.

"You know where your wife is?" Mackay said.

"Get out of here." Perkins reached for the bell button.

"Spira was murdered tonight. Shot stone cold dead!"

Perkins lay back. He closed his eyes, a sudden weariness on his face that had grown thin in the hospital. As thin as his wife's face now. His voice was bitter.

"Did you kill him too? To show how dangerous it all is?"

Mackay sat down, crossed his muscular legs, one leg slowly swinging in the hospital room.

"I just came from your house. Your wife isn't there. You know where she is? You ever know where she is?"

"I don't chain her to the bed."

"Maybe you should, be a man. Where do people like you crawl from, find your damned crazy ideas? You know who Burt Tarcher is?"

"No. Should I?"

"Your wife does. She's been seeing a lot of him. A lover, maybe, or something else?"

Perkins opened his eyes. Slowly, the eyes resisting as if they didn't want to see Mackay or even the light.

"Maybe a hired gunman? A killer for Stewart and Spira?"

"If you think so, why don't you tell the police not me?"

"I have, and I will. What are you going to do?"

Perkins closed his eyes again. "Build my house."

"Not in this town."

Silence hung in the room, but a hospital is never silent.

Coughing somewhere, harsh and endless. Nurse's heels on the hard floors. Machines pulsing. The low voices of doctors.

"Why don't you get out of this town, Perkins?" Mackay said. His leg swung faster. "Go as far as you can. We don't want you here. You're a cancer, you upset the balance, you destroy the clean cells. A cancer has to be cut out. Two dead because of you and that shit you call a house! Two now, and who knows how many more? Homes ruined, lives busted up, investments lost because you have to set yourself arrogantly apart from good, true, decent people! Goddamn it, Spira was a good man! Get out of this town! As far away as you can get!"

When Mackay stopped, breathing hard from the tirade, he saw Perkins lying there looking at him. Nothing else, just lying there looking at him without any expression at all. Mackay stood up.

"I'm not kidding, Perkins," he said. "I'm doing you a favor. Two favors—Burt Tarcher, the Fig Tree Motel."

He walked out of the neat hospital room.

John Perkins went on looking at where Mackay had been, silent and pale, his arm in its sling moving slowly with his breathing.

18

Beckett left his car on Beacon Road. There was light in one second-floor window of the big white house, and somewhere at the rear. He moved silently under the trees, and looked in at the kitchen window.

Grace Mackay sat at the kitchen table with a cup of tea. She wasn't drinking the tea. She was staring straight ahead, an emptiness on her young face. There was no sign of anyone else. Beckett returned to the front, rang at the door.

"Mr. Beckett, isn't it?" Grace Mackay said, smiled at him. "I'm sorry, Bill isn't home."

"You know where he is?"

"No. He has his work."

"Yeh," Beckett said. "Is Mrs. Stewart home?"

"No, I'm sorry again."

"I'd like to look at her room."

"Well . . . Bill always says—"

"There was another murder tonight, Mrs. Mackay."

Her eyes were stricken. "Oh, no! I'm . . . who was it?"

"George Spira."

"I . . . I didn't know him. I . . . yes, go on up."

In the large master bedroom where there were only woman's clothes in the closets, Beckett went through all the closets and drawers. He had the gray button in his hand.

Because he had remembered at once that the first time he had met Barbara Stewart in this house the day after Stewart's death she had been wearing a gray pantsuit with cloth-covered buttons the size of a nickel.

He didn't find the suit.

He went through the other bedrooms except the one where the two children were playing some quiet game. There was no gray suit. He went back down to the kitchen.

"Is there a laundry room, Mrs. Mackay?"

"Just through that door."

He found the gray suit in the dryer. A wash-and-wear wool blend. He took it out. One button was missing. The second button from the top of the jacket, and it was the button he had found. There were no stains on the suit, not now.

"When did you see Mrs. Stewart last?" he asked.

Grace Mackay thought, sipped her tea. "Late this evening. She went out at lunchtime, came back, and sat out there under that tree again all afternoon. She had some phone calls, and ate dinner. The children and I went to a movie at six-thirty. When we returned about eight-forty she was gone."

It had been eight-thirty P.M. when Beckett had found George Spira, and about nine when the coroner had reported. So as close as it could be figured now, Spira had been shot between seven-thirty and eight-thirty, probably closer to eight. Plenty of time for Barbara Stewart to shoot him, and come home to change her clothes.

"Did she say anything about where she was going?"

"No. One of her phone calls was from Tom McKay."

Beckett took the gray pantsuit with him. The garage

doors were open, only the old Cadillac inside. He drove north back to Fremont.

There was no light aboard the *Paloma*, but the cabin was open, and the bunk had been turned down as if McKay had been ready to sleep. An empty Scotch bottle stood on the cabin table.

The night of the marina was quiet and still. Only the creak of the boats, the voices of a party on one boat, and music that carried from the Golden Hind Lounge in the row of shops near the breakwater. Beckett walked to the lounge. Tom McKay sat at the end of the small bar, alone among the low-talking couples at the tables. Beckett sat down, ordered a beer.

"There's been another murder."

"Who?"

"George Spira."

"My God." McKay drank. "When?"

"Somewhere around eight o'clock tonight."

McKay pushed his glass to the bartender, waited for the Scotch to be poured and the water added.

"He was asking questions," McKay said. "Playing policeman."

"I don't know what he was playing," Beckett said. "You're in a drinking mood tonight."

"Sometimes it gets lonely on the boat."

Beckett listened to the muted music of the dim lounge. "You do what you want, are in control of your life. Drinking could mean you have a problem."

"Nothing's ever exactly the way you want it, is it?" McKay studied his own reflection in the bar mirror. "Any idea who killed him?"

Beckett said, "Maybe it's time you stopped holding back, told me what you've been hiding." He showed McKay the brass disk. "Yours, isn't it? I cabled Papeete.

146

They tell me it's probably a key tag from some sailors' hotel or old ship's cabin. Popular down there as souvenirs.''

McKay took the disk. ''Where did I lose it?''

''In the trees when you were watching the Stewart house the night Gordon Stewart was killed.''

McKay said nothing. The canned music stopped in the lounge as the piano player sat down at the piano bar across the room.

Beckett said, ''You asked me *when* Spira was killed. Why? Was Barbara Stewart on your boat sometime to-night?''

''Is she your suspect?'' McKay drank again.

The people moved from the bar to the piano bar, leaving only McKay, Beckett, and one solitary drinker.

''She was here,'' McKay said. ''About nine o'clock.''

With a flourish, the piano player launched into a medley of popular songs from the last decade and before.

''She was restless,'' McKay said. ''She talked about an old boyfriend, about her father, about the princess she'd been in her father's house. She seemed to be back in the past in her mind.''

''Okay,'' Beckett said, ''now tell me the rest. What did she really talk about when she visited you before Stewart's death? What did you see when you watched the house that night?''

The piano player was working his way back to World War II. Memories for some, nostalgia for others. McKay heard memories.

''I hadn't really talked to her for twenty years. It was something of a shock when she appeared on the boat that day.'' McKay drank. ''You're right, she was torn up, worried. She did talk about the cube house and Stewart. She said she wished that Stewart wouldn't defend the *awful* house, that it was going to ruin them all. She was shaken, *sorry* about everything. She said that Stewart was right and they were wrong. She didn't say who *they* were, though, rambled about not being close to Stewart.''

The piano player was hammering out "Remember Pearl Harbor." McKay seemed to be remembering. "I've often wondered how she came to marry Gordon Stewart, they weren't really much alike. He wasn't her kind of man any more than I was. I suppose she saw only his gentle ways. Unassertive, meek. The weak masculinity, and missed the iron in him, the strong principles.''

"She likes weak men?"

"She likes strong men, but she needs weak ones. A conflict. She needs weak men but rejects them, marries strong men and tries to make them weak." McKay smiled thinly. "My own story.''

Beckett said, "Why did you watch the house that night?"

"She wasn't very coherent that day, I got worried. So I went to the house, but I couldn't go in. I saw Stewart come home about eleven-thirty. Around two-thirty the telephone rang in the house for a long time. No—''

"You didn't see Hansen come to pick her up?"

"No," McKay said, "and no one answered the telephone. A car drove up about three A.M. I went closer, but all I could see was the car parked near the garage until around three-thirty when a man and a woman came from behind the garage and got into the car. The man seemed to be helping the woman walk, and they drove off. Around dawn another car arrived, then left again after maybe ten minutes.''

"Why did you hold all that out, McKay?"

McKay drank, watched the piano player. "I don't know. To try to protect her, I suppose. Now—?"

"Now there's another death that might have been prevented if you'd told us what you knew," Beckett said. He

148

finished his one beer. "Where did she go tonight? After she was here."

"I told her to go home. She said she would."

"She didn't."

"Maybe she did," McKay said. "Maybe she really went 'home.' Her mother still lives in San Vicente, I don't know where."

*

In the comfortable living room, Barbara Stewart sat smiling at the older woman.

"Can I have my room tonight?"

"It's not made up, you didn't say you were coming."

"I'll make it up, Mother," Barbara said. On the couch she swung her long leg restlessly. "I remember when Dad had it built for me. I was twelve or thirteen."

"Too old to share a room with Sammy anymore."

"My own room with my own bathroom."

Her mother laughed. "You guarded it like a dragon. No one was allowed in, not even me."

"I loved it. We had a happy home, didn't we?"

"Paul wasn't so damned happy. He was furious. He was the oldest, thought it should have been his room with the private bathroom."

Her mother laughed again. She was a sturdy old lady in her late sixties with lively eyes and hair almost white. Bigger than Barbara, in a long red robe with a high neck, she lit a small, thin cigar and waved the match out.

"Are you all right, Barb?"

"All right? Yes, I'm fine."

"They haven't found who did it, learned what happened?"

"Not yet." Barbara hunched forward on the couch as if cold in the warm room. "Do you remember Jim Fitch? A handsome boy, wasn't he? Big and confident. I wonder where he is?"

"He's still right here, you know that. Took over his dad's hardware store on Cota Street. He was too young for you."

"Or Sally Greer?" Barbara said. "We were so close all through high school and college. I haven't seen her in years. Not after she married Hal Greer."

"She's a widow now. Still lives there on Mission."

"Her old family house? Yes, I forgot."

Her mother blew the cigar smoke. "Are you sure you're all right?"

"I said I was!" Barbara snapped, frowned. "Why?"

"You haven't talked about those people in twenty years. You sound like someone who moved a thousand miles away. But Fremont's not thirty miles away, and you never tried to keep in touch with any of them."

"No," Barbara said. "Thirty miles?"

Still hunched forward, her arms hugging herself in the room that wasn't cold, she didn't see the tall, gray-haired man come into the living room from the back of the house. The man raised an eyebrow, her mother winked at him, and Barbara looked up.

"This is Fred Walsh, Barb," her mother said. "My daughter Barbara, Fred."

"Hello, Barbara," Walsh said, strode forward to shake hands.

Barbara shook hands, but sat staring up at the tall old man without speaking. Walsh smiled, spoke over his shoulder.

"I think I'll go up to bed, Sarah. Have a good talk."

He patted the older woman, and went out of the room. Barbara watched him go. Her mother smoked her thin cigar.

"He's living here?" Barbara said.

"Sometimes," her mother said. "When I want him to.

150

He's quite a man. Been everywhere, done everything, and doesn't have a dime to show for it. But what stories, and what life!"

"Mother, you're almost seventy!"

"Sixty-eight, and he's sixty-five, and it's not your business. It's still my house, and I'm not ready for burial."

"Yes," Barbara said. She stood up. "I'm sorry, Mother."

She stood uncertain in the comfortable room, looking at it like a stranger. Then she walked out of the room and out of the house. Her mother tamped out her cigar in an ashtray, not looking at the cigar but toward the closed outside door.

*

Prosecutor Charles Tucker paced his small study.

"At least I couldn't have killed Spira," he said. "I was making a speech at eight o'clock. So now Hoag moves into high gear, goes after them all?"

"Yeh," Beckett said, held his hot coffee in both hands.

"But you think the Stewart woman? On both?"

"That button could have gotten into Spira's car some other way, or at some other time. It could have been another woman McKay saw that night at the garage. She could be running off for another reason."

Tucker sat down. "Could she lift a big man like Spira?"

"No, but McKay admits she could probably have dragged him. She's a distance swimmer, has a senior lifeguard rating."

"Have you discussed it with Hoag?"

Beckett sipped at his coffee. "Not yet. I'm going to hold off. There're still things I don't like the feel of, Charley, something off key."

"Then you better find her fast," Tucker said.

"Tomorrow, or I'll turn it over to Hoag," Beckett said.

*

There was light in the house on Mission Street in San Vicente. A chunky woman in her mid-forties answered the door.

"Sally?" Barbara Stewart said.

The woman peered out. Her eyes widened. "Barbara? My God, come in! What a surprise! How long . . . Oh, I'm sorry. I heard about your husband. What a terrible thing! You know I lost my husband too? A year ago now. Not like yours, of course. I mean . . . have they caught who did it?" She chattered on as she led Barbara through a shabby, cluttered living room into a kitchen full of dirty dishes. "Don't even look at this place. I've just gone to pot since Hal died. I know it's terrible, but with the kids gone, and Hal . . . I'll make some coffee. Gosh, you look great. What a tan. I wish I got out more."

Barbara sat at the kitchen table. When the coffee was ready, Sally sat down.

"It's been a long time, Barb."

Barbara said, "Do you remember all the overnights we had here? In your room? Wondering about everything?"

"And your room too. Giggling maniacs. Before boys, eh?"

"They were good times," Barbara said. She became silent. "Can I sleep here tonight, Sally? Just tonight?"

"Here? Sure, but why not with your mother?"

"My mother has company."

Sally grinned. "She's quite a girl. Imagine!"

"I don't think I could," Barbara said.

"No. Well, I heard you were in real estate now?"

"All grub and grab and cheat and lie," Barbara said. "All dirt and ugliness. I hate it. I hate myself."

"Barb? Are you okay?"

"I'm sorry. I must be tired. Would you mind if I—?"

"Of course not. We can talk tomorrow. We're not those

152

giggling little all-night virgins anymore, are we?"

Alone in the small bed in the borrowed nightgown, Barbara lay with her eyes open, listening. As if she could hear that far-off, happy giggling of two young girls in this other room of her childhood. She closed her eyes, imagined she was back in those days, in those rooms, a virgin again.

19

Beckett found the big brick house set back behind a high hedge and a well-tended lawn on the upper East Side of San Vicente. Only a battered red Mustang stood in the side driveway in the early morning. A tall, gray-haired older man opened the door.

"I'm looking for Mrs. Sarah Halliday?" Beckett said.

"You've found her." The man called back into the house. "Sarah! A gentleman to see you. You've been holding out on me!"

There was a snorting laugh from somewhere inside, and the gray-haired man smiled.

"In the breakfast room," he said, and vanished.

Beckett entered a light, airy room of bamboo furniture and the full morning sun through a wall of French doors. The woman at the breakfast table wore a long red robe, had white hair and alert eyes, and was smoking a thin little cigar with her coffee. She waved Beckett to a seat. "Coffee?"

"Thanks," Beckett said, sat down. "My name is Beckett, Mrs. Halliday, from the County Prosecutor's Office."

"Then I expect you really want to see Barbara."

"Is she here?"

"She was last night, but she didn't stay." She dropped two lumps of sugar into her coffee. "Is there some problem?"

"You have any reason to think so?" Beckett said.

Sarah Halliday surveyed her bright backyard through the French doors. There were no curtains on the doors as if she loved the light.

"Barbara was agitated last night, restless," she said. "She talked too much about people she hasn't seen or cared about for years."

The older woman gestured with her hands as she talked. Large hands, wrinkled, but as expressive as her eyes.

"There was another murder last night," Beckett said. "Did Barbara mention a George Spira, talk about her real estate work?"

Sarah Halliday shook her head. "She talked about a boy she had been going to marry after college, her best friend when she was a girl, and her room."

"Room?"

The mother nodded. "When she was twelve or so her father had a room built for her. It was away from the other bedrooms, had a small private bathroom, and she loved it. Her domain, separate and special."

"Privileged and isolated?" Beckett said.

Sarah Halliday laughed. "Her brothers thought so, especially my older son Paul. She was always battling with the boys anyway. One long competition to do better than the others. The boys live away now, or they'd probably all still be at it."

"Being successful is important to her? Making money?"

"Not success or money *per se*, but winning at whatever she does, being *better*."

"Is that why she married successful men?"

155

"Probably," Sarah Halliday said, "although I'm not sure Barbara ever really married anyone. I'm not sure many people do today. Not marriage as I know it. My husband and I understood each other. We knew how to get along, how to please each other, what each of us needed, and we tried to do it. That's considered wrong today, doing what you may not really want to do to please someone else so he or she will please you. Perhaps that's a gain, for women especially, but I'm not so sure."

Beckett seemed to think. "Did she say anything about someone wanting her money? Now or later?"

"No. You think that could have something to do with Gordon's death? Or this Mr. Spira?"

"I don't know, Mrs. Halliday. Do you have any idea where she went after she left here last night?"

Sarah Halliday shook her head. "The friend she talked about, Sally Greer, lives near here on Mission Street, but that's all I can suggest."

Beckett thanked her, got up. She watched him.

"Do you suspect my daughter of killing her husband?"

"Could she have, Mrs. Halliday?"

"She could never kill anyone intentionally, by design."

"I'll keep that in mind," Beckett said.

*

Colonel Benjamin Hillock splashed soda into his bourbon. "You're sure you won't have anything, Mr. Tarcher?"

"Too early for me, Colonel," Burt Tarcher said. He lounged back on Hillock's living room couch. "The younger generation just can't keep up with you old soldiers."

"You emphasize *soldier*. Were you in the service too?"

"Good Christ, no! No more draft, thank God."

Hillock carried his drink to a high-backed armchair, sat eyeing Tarcher. "You know, it's that attitude that leads to

156

domination by the military. The citizen army has always been the backbone of free people, the curb on military rule. Look at South America with its professional armies loyal to their generals more than their countries. You liberals, or leftists, or whatever you really are, ought to think about that." He drank. "Even the socialists conscript citizen armies."

"So you've heard about me and my magazine?" Tarcher smiled.

"Hoag told me. It's not going to help the Perkinses."

Tarcher shrugged. "My stories won't help your side. I've got one story that especially won't help you."

"What story?"

"About those houses down at your old command."

Hillock nodded. "And you plan to print that story?"

"I really don't want to, you know?"

"What do you want?"

"Well, I'll level with you, Colonel," Tarcher said seriously, his voice sincere. "You know I've got a good line on the cube house story through the Perkinses. But I like to do a complete job, and I need a line to the other side, your side. All the info on the Mar Vista people's actions. If I had that, I just wouldn't have space for your little deal, you see?"

"Yes," Hillock said, "I see."

Tarcher sat back. "I could play down that maybe you didn't want the cube house thing to go to court and draw attention to you. People might get the idea that you wanted Stewart out of the way, and maybe Spira. I mean, he was checking real estate records, you know? If you got charged about those houses down at your base, and they proved you used the profits to buy the house here, you might lose this house. You're a trained soldier. You know guns, and violence, and are trained to act, right?"

"A straight deal, eh?"

Tarcher smiled. "It looks fair to me."

"Except," Hillock said calmly over his bourbon, "you made two mistakes. First, I doubt that they can prove anything on those houses, and I'm sure that they won't really try—good of the service, you know? Second, I don't deal with punk blackmailers. Not ever."

"Now listen—!"

"Get out of this house right now, or I'll break your arms."

Tarcher got up so fast he stumbled. He glared at Hillock, and then hurried out. Hillock sat there until he heard Tarcher's car drive away. He got up and mixed a fresh bourbon and soda. His wife came out of the next room.

"Maybe you should have made that deal," she said. "What do we owe these people here?"

"I never wanted to build those houses, did I, Pat? Your idea. I owed you for all those empty years of army camps, for the lousy life of an army wife. But they'll sweep it under the rug, they have to. Only I think we better get out of here. I think I know a buyer."

"Sell?" Patricia Hillock said. "Leave here?"

"At only a small loss, I hope."

She stared at him. He went on drinking his bourbon.

*

Sally Greer seemed ready to cry. "She slept here last night, Mr. Beckett, but she was gone when I got up. She didn't even leave a note. Just made the bed, folded my nightgown up on it, and went."

She wiped her eyes. "I was planning a special breakfast the way we always did on overnights when we were kids. Fresh juice, ham, eggs, hot muffins . . ."

"She talked about those overnights? When you were kids?"

158

Sally Greer nodded. "Happy days, she said, and they were. For both of us. But—" She looked at Beckett. "Something's wrong, isn't it? I sensed it last night."

"Why?" Beckett said.

"She came here to sleep, when her mother's house is a few blocks away," she said. "We were best friends all the time we were young, but after she married Tom McKay and moved to Fremont I didn't see her more than every few years. At big parties. She hadn't been in this house for twenty years. Why now?"

"Walking through her past?" Beckett said.

Sally Greer wandered about her cluttered kitchen, last night's dishes still in the sink. The ham and eggs were out on a counter, the ham already dry and curling.

"You know, she didn't say a word about her husband," Sally Greer said. "I tried to talk about him, sympathize, but she just didn't respond. As if he wasn't important at all."

Beckett watched her wander. "You don't sound surprised."

"I don't think Barbara ever really liked marriage," she said. She turned to look at Beckett, her eyes defiant, as if expecting to be challenged. "She was going to marry Jim Fitch after college when I married Hal. She didn't, I never knew why. I know they'd been to bed, so it wasn't sex, not physical trouble anyway."

Her face became distant, her eyes abstracted. Remembering and seeing. Beckett waited in the neglected kitchen.

"She said something last night. It—" She took a deep breath. "When we were teenagers she was so fastidious. She hated 'smells,' 'gunk,' 'dirt.' It was all so ugly. When we talked about boys, all of us, Barb would say that she never wanted a husband but she wanted a child. A neat trick, she'd say, joking, but sometimes I thought she wasn't joking."

159

Beckett said, "What did she say last night?"

"I asked her about her real estate work. She said it was all grub and grab and cheat and lie. All dirt and ugliness. She hated it, and hated herself."

"She said it about her real estate business?"

Sally Greer nodded. "But, somehow, I think she meant more than business. She sounded so full of disgust. With herself."

Beckett was silent in the grubby kitchen as the widow went on wandering around touching things but not seeing them.

"But you don't know where she could be now?"

"No. Maybe she went to see Jim Fitch. As you said, she seems to be walking through her past."

*

The late morning fog shrouded the beach and hid the sea outside the window of Judy Muldahr's beach house. Sitting in her living room, Judy stiffened as a car stopped behind the house. She listened to the foghorn on the distant breakwater. Her door opened and closed.

"So you went to Maxwell Bowman," Bill Mackay said.

He walked past her and looked out at the fog.

"Bowman said you were going to Spira too," Mackay said. "That was dumb; Spira was killed last night. Going to Bowman was dumb too."

"I didn't go to Spira," Judy said.

"Who knows?" He turned now. "You told Bowman I planted that memo to try to frame the Perkinses. You told him maybe I killed Stewart for the same reason."

"You could have," Judy said. "You've almost dared them to prove you did. Maybe if they know about the memo they can."

"And you can prove I faked the memo?"

Her face was impassive. "You told me to tell Beckett that

160

Mr. Stewart was going to quit the case. You told me not to let him see the files that first day. You used my keys to get into the office and type the memo."

"Is that all?" Mackay's voice was light, easy.

"Mr. Stewart never typed a personal memo like that," Judy said, "and when I told you that Beckett had found the memo you knew it had been typed before I ever mentioned that."

Mackay looked out the window at the fog again. "You'll tell them all that?"

"I can, and I can tell your wife about us," Judy said. She stood, joined him at the window to look out at the fog that was slowly drifting out to sea. "We're two of a kind, Bill. I want you full time, just for me, or I want enough money to get out of this town and live somewhere in style. One or the other. It's up to you."

"You think you're like me, Judy? A tough team?"

"I know I am."

A thin sun seemed to drift through the fog and shine on her heavy face and black hair.

"No, you're not like me. You're over your head, out of your depth. You picked the wrong man, and you're dumb. I don't care what you tell my wife. She knows me, I do what I want to do. Anywhere, anytime, with anyone."

"Then she won't stop you. I won't let you walk away from me, Bill. Not me."

"Yes you will."

He hit her in the face. She was flung back against a wall of the small room, almost fell. He hit her again. And again. Blood spurted from her broken nose. Her lips were split and her mouth a hole of blood. She screamed. Mackay hit her. She fell, moaning, cowering on the floor against the wall. He bent and hit her once more. As hard as he could.

"No one threatens me," he said, his face down close to

161

hers, close to the blood and bone. "No one tells me what I'm going to do. No one goes to the police. So long, Judy."

*

The Buddhist temple was on the lower west side of San Vicente. A low, serene building on a narrow lot in the poorest area of the city, as delicate as a doll's house among the squat stucco bungalows of the old section.

Barbara Stewart sat alone in the austere silence of the long, narrow, muted interior. Two monks in saffron robes, their heads shaved, chanted cross-legged.

Barbara Stewart sat with her head bent, her eyes closed, her lips moving soundless. She still wore the high-necked navy blue dress, wrinkled now.

Worshippers came and went softly.

No one approached Barbara Stewart.

No one spoke to her or looked at her.

After a time, still motionless, she opened her eyes and looked at the people who came to pray, to meditate, to chant their mantras. Each isolated, and all one.

Barbara Stewart seemed to watch them with a sadness, a sense of pain on her long, tanned face, an endless despair.

She sat in the temple for some hours.

It was afternoon before she stood up stiffly, put on her shoes at the door, and left.

20

An old-fashioned bell tinkled as Beckett opened the door of Fitch's Hardware Emporium on Cota Street. Cluttered with open bins, barrels, and antique many-drawered cabinets, the shop was something out of the last century when San Vicente had been a sleepy Mexican town only recently invaded by the gringos.

It was a fake.

Narrow, it occupied the entire building through to the next street, and behind the antique decoration computerized modern efficiency offered every doodad of plastic hardware and houseware. Jim Fitch laughed.

"You like the bell, the old 'emporium'? My own gimmick. Everything's got to be a gimmick today, nostalgia and all that. The honest, peaceful past. They love it, as long as I've got all the latest junk they want, and a computer to keep an eye on the profits."

"People buy this kind of fakery?" Beckett wondered.

"People buy anything if you shout loud enough, and tell them everyone else is buying it," Fitch said.

"You're a cynic," Beckett said.

"You get that way. Come on into the office."

Fitch was a medium-sized, mediumly dressed, comfortable-looking man in his mid-forties, and in his small office he lit a pipe. There were rows of TV monitors on the wall that showed every corner of the store. There was also a color TV, a stereo, and a home bar. Fitch wasn't thinking of any of that.

"Barbara?" he said, shook his head. "I heard about her husband. The paper said maybe murder. You people sure?"

"You don't think it was murder?"

"I'd have put my money on suicide for him."

"You knew Stewart?"

"I knew Barbara." Fitch puffed to keep his pipe lit. "He was married to her."

"Have you seen her recently? Say, this morning?"

"Christ, no. I haven't seen Barb in twenty-five years. Oh, I've bumped into her, sure, but we haven't talked since the day she walked out on me."

"Why did she walk out?"

Fitch looked at his pipe, it had gone out. "She never said. Just that she couldn't marry me, probably couldn't marry anyone."

"But she did. Twice. Did that surprise you?"

Fitch relit his pipe. "Yes and no." He waved out the match, thoughtfully. "It's a long time ago, and I was a kid then, but it meant a hell of a lot then, and I've thought about it over the years. I guess I never stopped thinking about it."

He had the pipe going again. "She was my first time in bed, and I guess I was hers. The sex was real good—at first. Then she changed, began to pull away. Began to act like she hated it all. We were up in that room of hers one time, playing around and just about ready to make love, when she started to stare at me. Down there, you know? She sud-

164

denly said it was ugly, disgusting, like a skinned turkey neck."

Fitch shook his head, remembering that long ago moment. He sighed. "We never went to bed again except in the dark, and it wasn't the same any more. She seemed to need me, want me, and she seemed to want me to want her, admire her, chase her. She wanted the sex, but she'd pull away, turn off. It got to be a hassle every time I tried. More and more until she called it all off, and we never really saw each other again. I called her, she called me, but somehow we never got together. No real break, it just sort of faded out."

"And you didn't meet her again?"

"Once. I remember now. It was a year later, more. She was in the hospital. I visited her. She didn't really care.

"Why was she in the hospital?"

"I don't know for sure. Some kind of accident."

"What hospital?"

"Ward Memorial."

"Can you think of anywhere she might go if she was thinking about her past?"

"No," Fitch said. "Our part of the past ended just where I told you."

Beckett thanked him. Fitch nodded.

"When you find her, say hello," he said.

*

The doctor stepped back from the hospital bed, and nodded to Cathy Perkins. "He's doing fine. I'd say home tomorrow."

The doctor patted John Perkins before he left. Cathy smiled, kissed Perkins and promised to visit him again before dinnertime. Alone, his arm out of the sling for the first time since he'd been shot, Perkins looked out the hospital window at the afternoon sun of Fremont and the distant haze of fog waiting offshore to slip back over the land after dark.

The nurse came in, refilled his water glass.

"Everything all right? Comfortable?"

"Yes, fine," Perkins said.

The nurse scanned the room, nodded, and left. Perkins heard her enter the next room. He got out of bed.

Ten minutes later he stepped into a taxi waiting at the side of the hospital. He rode to his office building. He didn't go up, but went to his car in the parking lot and drove off again.

He drove through Fremont to the Fig Tree Motel. The clerk told him Burt Tarcher's room number. He knocked.

"Who is it?"

"John Perkins."

There was a silence. Perkins saw the curtain move on the front window. The door opened. "Come in then."

Perkins went inside. Tarcher scanned the area in front of the motel, closed the door, returned to the armchair he had been sitting in, and picked up his smoking cigarette. His foot tapped the floor. He wore his custom-made blue jeans, no shirt, and the heavy medallion dangled on his bare chest.

"What do you want, Perkins?"

"In what way do you know my wife?"

"In what way?" Tarcher smoked. "She didn't send you?"

"No." Perkins stepped closer to the nervous magazine man. He winced, and his hand moved toward the bulge of the bandage on his shoulder under his shirt. He forced the hand back to his side, his mouth a thin line in his soft, pale face. "Some people say you're Cathy's lover. Some say you're a hired gunman. What are you? How do you know my wife?"

"Jesus, who the hell have you been talking to?" Tarcher said. He crushed out his cigarette. "She's not my type, and

166

I don't know one end of a gun from the other."

Tarcher got up and began to pace the room as if his mind were on something a lot more important than John Perkins. He seemed to have forgotten Perkins was there.

"What is your business with her?" Perkins said. His pale face was drawn.

"What?" Tarcher stopped in the middle of the room. "Oh, hell, we made a deal for your story. The dream house, the establishment pressure, the trial, the whole shit."

"Story?" Perkins blinked at Tarcher.

"For *People's Voice* magazine. She sold me full rights for twenty thou' plus bonuses per day. Okay?"

Perkins walked out of the motel. Tarcher went on pacing.

*

Ward Memorial Hospital was a large collection of old and new buildings on the upper West Side of San Vicente. Beckett identified himself, asked for the administrator, and told him what he wanted.

"I could subpoena the records," Beckett said, "but time may be important. I don't need to read it, just ask some questions."

"This is official business, Mr. Beckett?" the administrator said, and when Beckett nodded he flicked his intercom and ordered the records. "Twenty-five years is a long time, but they should be on microfilm."

They were. The administrator inserted the film into a small desk reader, looked at Beckett.

"What was she in the hospital for? How long?"

"It was an emergency case from a private doctor. An accident. She was here three days."

"What kind of accident?"

"Drug poisoning, and that's all I can give you."

"Who signed her out? Paid?"

"She was twenty-one, paid and signed out herself."

"It could be awfully important," Beckett said.

The administrator switched off his reader. He sat back. "The doctor who sent her in was Dr. Matthew Schatz."

Beckett went to the nearest phone booth. Dr. Matthew Schatz, general surgeon, had his offices a block from the hospital.

The waiting room was crowded. Beckett explained his business to the receptionist. In a small, private office, Dr. Schatz swung back and forth in his chair. A big man in his fifties.

"I was a young G.P. then, didn't even know the girl," he said. "Is she in trouble?"

"Trouble or danger or both, I don't know. She's missing, there are two murders, and I need any leads to find her."

The doctor went on swinging. "It was an overdose of pills, Seconal. A boy she was with got her to me. I took her to the hospital and they pumped her out. That's it."

"An accidental overdose? Sleeping pills?"

"That's what they both said. She'd been drinking too. She was young, high-strung, hysterical. They were both scared to death, it looked honest to me. I reported it to the police. No one ever came back to me, except the boy, so I assume it was legitimate."

"Why did the boy come back?"

"He was my patient. He still is, or was, I haven't seen him for some time."

"Jim Fitch?"

"Edgar Johnson."

"You have his address?"

"My receptionist should have," Schatz said. "And let me know how it comes out. I've sometimes wondered what happened to that girl."

*

168

Phil Hansen was on the phone when Colonel Benjamin Hillock came into the bungalow office of Hansen Realty. Hansen waved him to a seat while he talked.

"I don't know where the hell she is. No, she didn't say a damn thing to me. Yeh, but Mackay hasn't seen her since yesterday, or so he says. You just take care of your paper work, and I'll try to find her." He hung up, sat tapping a pencil on the desk. He looked toward Hillock. "You don't happen to have seen Barbara Stewart today?"

"No. Is she missing?"

"She hasn't been around today."

"Just today?"

"Yeh," Hansen said, tapped the pencil, "probably nothing. Well," he took a breath, grinned, the eternal optimist, "you must have something else on your mind."

"Do you still have that buyer for my house?"

"You want to sell? Now?" Hansen sat up at the prospect of business, then his face clouded. "I don't know. The case isn't even in court, won't be until Perkins gets better and finds a lawyer. Who's going to buy now?"

"You said you had someone."

"Yeh." Hansen's eyes gleamed briefly. "But that was months ago. People are waiting to buy in Mar Vista now, you'd take a loss." He tapped the pencil again. "Of course, I might buy it myself, take a gamble we'll win the case."

"Pay me what I paid and you have a deal. No loss."

Hansen thought. "Done. Tomorrow?"

"I'll be here." Hillock got up.

"It's sort of sudden, isn't it?" Hansen said.

"Not really," Hillock said. "Tomorrow."

In a kind of reverie, Hansen sat there watching the closed door for some time. He looked at his phone, picked it up.

"Mrs. Mackay? Is your husband home? When do you expect him? Okay. Oh, has Barbara come home? What?

The police? Beckett? When? Yeh, thanks."

Hansen hung up slowly, his eyes worried.

*

The address the receptionist had given Beckett was a sleek apartment court on the west side of San Vicente. There was no answer at Edgar Johnson's apartment. Beckett rang the manager's bell. A small, fat man greeted him politely.

"Any idea where Edgar Johnson in apartment five is now?"

"At work, I hope."

"Where is that?"

"Some ad agency downtown. Don't know the name."

"When does he usually get home?"

"Hard to say. He's fancy-free, you know?" the manager said. "You could try the Pink Pelican around six."

Beckett drove down to Cuyama Beach, but the Stewart house was silent, with only the Cadillac in the garage. He drove back to Fremont and Judy Muldahr's beach house. Her car was there, but there was no response to his knock. He tried the door. It was unlocked.

There was no one in the tiny living room. No one in the kitchen. The beach through the high windows was chill and deserted as the heavy bank of fog lying offshore had started to move in again as evening approached.

Judy Muldahr was in the bedroom. She lay facing the wall.

"You don't answer your door?" Beckett said.

"Is there some law I have to? Is there some law that says you can walk in?"

"Yes, there is. Have you seen Barbara Stewart today?"

"No."

"Bill Mackay?"

"Go away." Her voice cracked. "Please."

170

Beckett heard the pain in the voice. He walked closer, saw the bandages on her face, the yellow stain of antiseptic.

"Mackay?" he said.

"I fell." Her voice low, not turning. "On the rocks going to surf. The doctor said I need to rest."

In the shade-drawn bedroom Beckett suddenly saw her as she was. For all her efficient facade, she was the plain, awkward girl you see on buses, on economy flights, on overnight train coaches with a baby and no man, while the smooth, confident girls with no more beauty travel in first class and ride in the Porsches on their way to ski resorts and exotic islands.

"He's using you," Beckett said. "What do you know that made him hurt you? What's he planning?"

"Please," she said.

"He'll come back."

"No," she whispered, "he won't come back."

A sense of despair in her voice. Mackay would not return. To love her or to beat her. She had lost him, and she would always travel third class.

21

Beckett stopped home for an early dinner, and it was six twenty-five P.M. when he entered the Pink Pelican in downtown San Vicente. All the tables were full, and two bartenders were working hard to serve the men two deep at the bar. There were no women. A big man approached Beckett.

"Mister," he said quietly. "I think maybe—"

Beckett showed his I.D. "I'm looking for Edgar Johnson."

The bouncer glanced around. "The small guy with the white hair at that corner table. This going to be noisy?"

"No," Beckett said. He pushed through the crowd of men to the table. Johnson was with a younger man. "Mr. Johnson? I'm Lee Beckett, County Prosecutor's Office. I'd like some help."

"Help? All right. Give me ten minutes, Sammy?"

The younger man left the table. Beckett sat down. Edgar Johnson was a small man in a neat business suit with clear blue eyes and a deep tan against his silver-gray hair.

"What kind of help, Mr. Beckett?"

"Have you seen Barbara Halliday lately?"

"Good grief!" Edgar Johnson said. He was about to laugh, then didn't. "You're serious? Seen Barbara? Why, I haven't seen her in, what, twenty-four years?"

"The time of her accident?"

Johnson studied Beckett. "Are you going to rake that up after all these years?"

"Is there anything to rake up?"

"I never knew," Johnson said. "Not for sure."

"Can you tell me what led up to it? The accident?"

"I suppose so. Why not?" Johnson looked around the crowded bar at all the men. "I was still trying then, you see. One hopes. She was on the rebound from Fitch, and we met. We got along nicely. Not too much bedroom, but that seemed to suit us both. I mean, I guess I was trying to work things out in my mind, and she wanted it when she wanted it but not too often. Then one day she suggested we get married."

Johnson's thin smile was resigned. "I suppose that was what did it for me. I was suddenly scared, and one night she caught me in the sack with a boy. She ran out. Next day she called me, almost incoherent. She'd overdosed on those pills. I got her to my doctor, and that was it. The end."

"You never saw her again?"

"No, I . . . Wait, yes I did. I'd almost forgotten." Johnson listened to the rising noise in the bar. "It was much later, after she'd divorced that older man and married the lawyer. I was living with someone, and she came knocking on my door. I wondered how she'd even found me, and I was worried—I remembered the last time she'd walked in on me. But she didn't even seem to notice. As if she were sleepwalking, almost in shock."

"Walking through her past?" Beckett said.

"Something like—" Johnson understood. "Is that what

173

she's doing now? Why you thought I might have seen her?''

''What happened that last time?'' Beckett said.

''She talked. About the past, us, her childhood, and her husband. She was full of anger, and yet full of guilt too.''

''Was it a suicide try? With those pills?''

''I don't know. I've thought about it, but I don't know.''

''Can you give me anything to help locate her?''

''I'm afraid not. We don't move in the same circles.'' He half smiled again. That resigned smile, neither apologetic nor defiant. Not sad, but not especially happy. ''You know, she was a turning point for me. I learned to accept what was and what is. I'm not sure she ever did.''

''How do you mean?'' Beckett said.

Johnson looked toward the young man he was with who was watching them from across the noisy room. ''She talked sometimes about her and Fitch. He was an ordinary young man who would have been a normal husband to a normal housewife, but a normal housewife was something she didn't want to be. I think she decided to marry me because I wasn't an ordinary young man, so probably wouldn't ask her to be an ordinary, normal housewife. But then she found out that I probably wouldn't be a normal husband either, and that was something she did want.''

They both sat and thought. Dark now outside the bar, and the noise grew more excited among the crowd of men.

*

Dorky's was an ordinary saloon in a bowling alley on the far west side of San Vicente. The jukebox was loud, and the customers knew each other. The young bartender called all the middle-aged women by their first names. They loved it.

Barbara Stewart sat at a table in the darkest corner far from the jukebox. She was drinking martinis.

''I've got a good husband,'' she said to the muscular young man. ''A good man. Yes.''

174

"They're hard to find," the young man said.

He was a stocky youth no more than twenty-three or so, in a thin windbreaker, T-shirt, and tight jeans. His name was Ted.

"I had a good husband," Barbara said. "I killed him. Poor Gordon, he had to put up with me all those years."

"Nice name, Gordon," Ted said. "You live around here?"

Barbara nodded. "Yes, I have my own room. A nice clean room. No one comes in unless I say so. I have to go home."

"Night's young," Ted said. "Ready for another?"

"Martini," Barbara said. "On the rocks. Very dry."

"My room's nice too," Ted said.

The waitress brought the martini and a beer for Ted. She picked up the money from in front of Barbara, winked at Ted.

"Just around the corner," Ted said. "We could take a six pack, maybe a bottle."

"A good man, strong, and look what I did to him," Barbara said. "Phil Hansen! Dirty . . . dirty. Look at me!"

"Hey, you look pretty good to me. You know?"

Ted grinned. His hand touched her under the table. Her thigh under her wool dress, and moved upward. He smiled into her face. She moved against his hand under the table. Her eyes half closed. She breathed.

"You're a hell of a good-looking woman," Ted said.

His hand moved higher. She closed her eyes, breathed softly in the dim bar. She drank, long drinks.

"Dirty," she said. "Like you. Poor Gordon."

"I like you a lot," Ted said.

Barbara sat there against his moving hand. Ted smiled.

*

Beckett found Bill Mackay alone at the rear of Senator

Eller's campaign headquarters in downtown Fremont. After eleven, Mackay was drinking a beer. The street outside was deserted.

"You work late. Have you seen your mother today?"

"No," Mackay said. "Why?"

"She seems to be missing. Since Spira was killed."

"Barbara kill anyone?" Mackay laughed.

"Then where is she?"

"That's her business, right?"

Beckett sat down facing the mustachioed hatchet man. Mackay drank his beer. He didn't offer Beckett a beer.

"Why did you beat Judy Muldahr?" Beckett said.

"Did someone beat Judy up?"

"She knew you faked that memo, planted it."

"Why would I do that?"

"To give the Perkinses a motive for killing your stepfather, keep the pot boiling. You pushed for murder from the start, even though it could still be suicide or an accident. You want it to be murder to put pressure on the community and the Perkinses. Anything to get them out. You don't even mind if people think you killed him."

Mackay's face settled into a fixed smile as Beckett talked. His eyes flat and as fixed as the smile.

"You *want* people to think you could have killed him," Beckett said. "You want the Perkinses suspected, yes, but yourself too. It makes you seem dangerous, a threat. It might scare the Perkinses and others into making a quick compromise to end the cube house. It builds up pressure against the cube house—it's behind all the trouble so we must get rid of it. It, and its owners, and anyone who defends them."

Mackay's smile never changed. "What about the Perkinses wanting to keep it all in turmoil? I know who that

176

Tarcher is now. His subversive rag wants to make all the trouble it can, and the Perkinses are being paid to keep it all going."

"You don't *know* that," Beckett said. "Cathy Perkins sold the rights to their story, nothing more. You don't know that they've done anything except fight for their house. You don't know if they had any reason to kill Stewart or Spira. You don't *know* anything."

"I know what they are!" Mackay said fiercely. "I know they're the enemy. Our enemy. They're dangerous, you hear? They're against all we believe and want!"

Beckett sat back. "You know they're bad, so they must be stopped no matter how? If you can't find proof, you create it. They're evil, but you don't have evidence, so you make evidence? You'll get them on something even if they didn't do what you get them on? Convict them of anything you can, true or not?"

"They did something!"

"And to get them lies are as good as the truth?"

Mackay opened another can of beer.

"And if we don't 'get' them for you?" Beckett said. "What do you do then?"

Mackay drank his beer. A car stopped outside and two men got out. They glanced into the headquarters, then walked away.

"Be careful from now on, Mackay," Beckett said.

"I'm always careful," Mackay said.

Beckett got up. "You can't tell me where your mother is?"

"You'll have to do your own work," Mackay said.

*

Barbara Stewart lay rigid in the crumpled bed. She could smell him. She could feel him naked against her thighs, against her breasts. She could feel his hard legs, sense the

177

shadow of his shoulders, touch the slope of his chest down to the flat belly and below.

She could feel his hands on her.

"You have to go home," she said in the dark room.

"No way, baby, no way." His thick voice. "Only the beginning."

He took her again. Slower this time, longer and deeper. She slid down into the depth of herself. She hated him. A dirty little room of stinking male clothes, old beer cans, spilled gin, soggy towels. She sank into the deep warmth.

"I have to go," she said.

She did not go. She lay against him. She kissed his chest, his sweat, his stink.

Later. Again.

She awakened. Hands on her breasts. The hoarse voice.

"You know, you're pretty good for an old broad. You got a lucky husband. All night, yeh? The whole way."

"Pig!" Barbara cried to the darkness. "Go home! Go home now! Go!"

"Baby, we're going—"

"Get out of my room! Get out!"

"Hey, whoa!"

She hit his chest. She scratched at him. He held her.

"Knock it off! Lady, this is my room. You—"

She lay rigid.

"You want to go home, you go home!"

She shuddered. "Yes, I'll go home. I have to go home. When I'm clean, I'll go home. I can tell, be clean, and go home. The truth."

He lay snoring among the dirty sheets when she staggered out into the night.

*

Beckett sat in his living room looking down at the dark city in the late night. Where was Barbara Stewart?

178

He called Sarah Halliday. Barbara had not come back. He called Tom McKay. She wasn't on the *Paloma*. He called the old house in Cuyama Beach. Grace Mackay answered. Barbara had not come home. He called Charley Tucker.

"No, I wasn't asleep, Lee." Tucker's voice was tired, worn. "I've been with Hoag. He's been hounding them all, trying to trace Spira's movements."

"What does he say?"

"Almost all of them could have done it. Perkins has left the hospital, his wife doesn't know where he is. Hoag says he's got good leads, expects to wrap it up soon."

"Meaning he's got nothing," Beckett said.

"Or less," Tucker said.

"Tell him to watch Mackay," Beckett said.

"I'll tell him."

Beckett sat in his silent living room for a long time watching the dark city.

22

The insistent ringing of his telephone awakened Beckett.

"Mr. Beckett? Sarah Halliday. She called me ten minutes ago. I don't know where from."

"I'll be right over."

The sun was up in the foothills, but the city below still lay under the low bank of morning fog. He warmed some coffee, had juice and a cup of yogurt, and drove down into the town. The fog seemed to recede before him, and a thin sunlight shined on the old brick house of Sarah Halliday. She was in the breakfast room again. She sat alone at the rattan table.

"She sounded quite calm, Mr. Beckett, even in good spirits. Too calm, perhaps. As if she had no more problems, no worries."

"But she didn't say where she was?"

"Only that she had something to do, and then would be home." Sarah Halliday watched a strident mockingbird out in her back yard through the French doors. "She told me to get her room ready."

"Here?"

180

Sarah Halliday nodded. "So it seemed."

"When she took those pills years ago, was it suicide?"

"We wondered." Her expressive hands were a question. "But she recovered so quickly, married Tom McKay soon after. Perhaps if she had stayed with Tom?"

"Mrs. Halliday, did something else happen soon after she married Gordon Stewart? Did she leave Stewart for a time?"

"Yes," Sarah Halliday said. "Bill was about six or so. I don't know how long she was gone, or where she went, or why. Only Gordon seemed to know anything and he never talked about it. Later, Barbara said only that she had been ill and in the hospital, and had then visited a friend in the mountains."

"What hospital and what friend?"

"St. Stephen's in Fremont, and the friend was a girl she had known in college, Marian Cross." The old woman took one of her small cigars from a box, lit it. "Barbara never spoke of those times in the hospital, not even to me. I doubt that anyone beyond myself, and Gordon, and perhaps Tom McKay know about them. I think Barbara would like it to remain that way."

"She said nothing specific about what she was doing?"

"No. But I do think I heard another voice when she was on the telephone. A woman's voice."

"Did you tell her I was looking for her?"

"No." She smoked her cigar. "She may need help. I want you to find her."

*

Cathy Perkins heard the key turn down in the front door of the cube house. In bed, she listened. Slow footsteps went into the living room below. Glass clinked. Cathy put on her robe and hurried down the narrow, circular stairs.

"Where have you been?" she said.

John Perkins turned to look at her. He held a glass.

"I've been frantic, John! The sheriff was here asking questions about Mr. Spira; I thought something had happened!"

Perkins drank. "I talked to Tarcher."

"All right, you talked to Tarcher." She sat down, her thin face set. "Now you know. I'm glad you know."

Perkins walked to the large front window. Below the fog was lifting rapidly from the city, moving back out to sea.

"Twenty thousand and bonuses. A lot of money," he said. "But we were fighting for a principle. For the right to build our own house how we wanted and where we wanted."

"And risked losing everything!"

"Principles usually involve risks," Perkins said.

"How much? We stood to lose all even if we won! Our way of life, our careers, our hopes, our peace! We have a right to the future we've planned."

"Without principles? By deceit? Deceit and greed?"

"That's the way the world is! We have to live in the world as it is, John, not as we wish it was."

"No, we have to fight to live our way, Cathy. For the freedom to do our own living."

"And have the privilege of working twice as hard and long as anyone else for half the reward! We live in the world with *them*, John, don't you see?"

"Yes," Perkins said. "I see now."

"Was it so wrong?" Cathy said, looked up at him. "To want something for us? I'm no different from anyone else, John."

"No," he said, "you're no different from anyone else."

He put the glass carefully on a table, and walked from the odd house with its cubes and windowless walls.

*

182

The administrator at St. Stephen's Hospital had no objections to cooperating with Beckett. He sent him to the record room.

Barbara Stewart had cut her wrists in the old house in Cuyama Beach eighteen years ago. She was in the hospital a week. A psychiatrist had certified her recovered after a severe temporary depression. There was no reference to the earlier "accident" in the records. She had been released to her husband and a Dr. Marian Cross.

Beckett went back to the administrator.

"Dr. Marian Cross. Does she still have an office here?"

"I don't know, Mr. Beckett. She's not an M.D., you see. A Ph.D. in psychology. I believe she operated a kind of rest clinic in the mountains in those days."

Beckett went to the telephone book. There was no office listing for a Dr. Marian Cross, and no Dr. Cross in Fremont. But there was a private residence for a Marian Cross. In San Vicente.

*

Bill Mackay looked from face to face in the study of Maxwell Bowman's ranch house. Through the window the blank wall of the cube house towered like some monolithic idol of a primitive culture. Mackay studied each of their faces in turn, like the commander of some dangerous mission looking for weakness.

"Then we're all set?" he said finally.

"Loaded and ready," the stocky one said.

Maxwell Bowman shifted restlessly in his chair. His old face twitched nervously.

"You're sure it's the only way?" Bowman said.

Mackay nodded. "The damned police aren't going to do anything. I haven't come up with evidence good enough to get them off their asses. It's time for direct action, before the whole thing gets lost in the murders. People are losing their anger over that damned house already."

"I don't know," Bowman said. "Maybe—"

"It has to be done, Bowman! For the whole community."

"No more talk, eh, Billy boy," the tall, wiry one said. "No more pussyfooting legal crap."

"Action for the troops," the stocky one said.

Mackay nodded. "What's it going to be, Bowman? If you're too scared, we can move without you."

"Is there any way I can get out, Mackay?" Bowman said. "If I don't go along, I still hired you."

"That you did, and I promised results." He studied them all once more. "Tonight?"

"I'll drink to that," the stocky one said.

When Mackay and his two cronies had gone, Maxwell Bowman remained sitting in the study. His wife came in.

"Estelle?" Bowman said. "Why don't you go and visit your sister? You haven't seen her for some time."

"That would be nice, but I can't. We're electing a new president at the Native Daughters tomorrow. I have to be there."

"Yes," Bowman said. "Of course."

He got up, made himself a whisky and water, and sat down again.

＊

Marian Cross was a tall, broad-shouldered woman in her mid-forties. Her face was long and severe, and her dark hair was cut short and straight. In the early afternoon she wore a pair of gray slacks and a mannish tweed jacket over a button-down shirt. She nodded Beckett to a chair in a book-lined study cluttered with work-in-progress manuscripts.

"I mostly write now. Nearly as rewarding, and a lot less agonizing." She had controlled gray eyes. She sat with her

184

legs crossed. "Barbara said nothing about the prosecutor."

"She's here?"

"She was," she said. "Before I say more, I'd like to know the situation. It's her husband?"

"Him, and a man named Spira," Beckett said, and told her the circumstances of the deaths of Gordon Stewart and George Spira. He told her about the cube house, the gray button, and Barbara's running off. Marian Cross listened thoughtfully.

"All because of one odd house? It's quite amazing what people will become violent over, isn't it?" She thought about it. "Of course, it's not the house, it's the threat it represents to them. They feel threatened." She thought again. A person who lived by thought. "It seems, then, that she wasn't at home when her husband died, and a button can be lost in many ways. She talked about her husband last night, but said nothing about the other man, and she really didn't seem to be running away. More like she was searching toward something. I'd say you have very little to base an accusation on."

"I didn't say we were accusing her, Doctor, and I know how little I have. What I really have is a feeling, you know? A shadow in the back of my mind. That's why I have to find her."

She shook her head. "I don't know, Mr. Beckett. She said nothing last night that appears to bear on your problem. She came as a friend, nothing more."

"But you know more," Beckett said. "You're her friend, you treated her the time she cut her wrists."

Marian Cross was silent in the study. "Only casual friends, not close. At the time she was in the hospital she had me called and I took her to the mountains to recuperate. After that we saw each other from time to time—as friends, and, I suspect, without her family knowing. I think she came to me when she was disturbed, but she never said that, and it was never on a professional basis. She's too proud to admit needing help, and much too private a person ever to ask for it.''

"Yet she came to you last night," Beckett said.

"I had the impression that I was a last refuge, she had run out of places. Apparently she had been with some casual man. She was full of guilt and disgust. Disgust for herself, for everything. She seemed to be trying to make some decision, a bit vague, distracted. But this morning she was in quite good spirits. She called her mother, we had breakfast, and she left. She talked about nothing important at breakfast—our college days, her business, the past, my books.''

"What did she say about her real estate business?"

"She seemed disgusted with it too."

"Yeh," Beckett said. Now he thought for a time. "That *was* a suicide try eighteen years ago?"

"Yes."

"Is she a suicidal personality?"

She fixed her gray eyes toward her shelves of books. It was a question she didn't like or want to answer. "She has a strong sense of personal worth, even of superiority. She sees the world as crass, dirty. Human needs are ugly. She hates those needs. But she *has* those same needs too. She loathes the dirty world, but cannot help being part of it, so loathes herself. And such a person can seek ugliness, degrade any relationship to prove to herself how right she is.''

"I'm gonna hate myself in the morning for what I'm doing tonight," Beckett said. "All of us, but she exaggerates it?"

"We survive the feeling because our direction is toward the world. Her direction is away from the world. To remain untouched." Marian Cross moved almost painfully in her desk chair. "She functions because it usually satisfies her self-hate to *know* that the world is ugly. I expect she lives a crippled life, but gets by. Only something can happen to make her guilt rise so sharply that she can suddenly no longer permit herself to live with herself. Call it a psychic scream."

"A trigger," Beckett said.

"If you like, and no one else can know what or when. It's inside her, irrational."

"Could she commit murder?"

"I don't think so," Marian Cross said.

But Beckett heard a faint doubt in the words. A question. He waited.

"Possibly," she said, "if her guilt became so huge that she couldn't stand to think that someone else knew, she might kill to save that person from having to live with her guilt. An act of mercy. Twisted, but real." She sat there as if listening to her own words. "Does any of that help you?"

"Yeh, I think it fills in a picture."

She nodded. Beckett waited. Again he sensed something else, something more on Marian Cross's mind.

She said, "In her rambling last night she did say that, besides her father, she had known two good men in her life. She had married them both, and failed them both. She had to make that up to them, tell them, before she could go home."

"Stewart's dead," Beckett said.

"But I believe the first husband is still alive."

"Yeh," Beckett said. "He's alive."

23

In the late afternoon sun, Tom McKay stood on the deckhouse of the *Paloma* waving frantically as Beckett left the marina parking lot. Beckett hurried to the boat.

"She was here!" McKay jumped down to the deck. "Five hours ago! I tried to call you, but your office didn't know where you were!"

Beckett climbed aboard. "Where is she now?"

"I wish I knew! I tried to follow her, but I lost her."

"Follow her? Why?"

"She acted as if she were going to do something. Something urgent, secret!"

"Do what?"

"I don't know, damn it!" McKay glared. "You think I'd be waiting here if I did?"

"I don't know what you'd do," Beckett snapped. "I'm not a cop, I don't have a radio car. Why didn't you call the police or Hoag?"

"She's not a criminal! I don't trust Hoag or the police. I wanted help for her, not police chasing her!"

"All right, calm down," Beckett said. "Exactly what did

188

she say? You think she's going to do something dangerous?"

McKay paced the deck, waved his arms in his sailor's sweatshirt. "She said she was going home, but she had one more thing to do. She was going to clean it up, balance the books! She made it sound like something *final*. She was calm, cheerful, almost sexy to me. Playful. It scared me."

"That's all she said?"

McKay laughed. It wasn't a happy laugh. "She said she had come to tell me I'd been a good husband, I was a good man. God, twenty years ago, and she seemed to think it was important to tell me that! She said she'd hurt me, but she hadn't been able to help that, and she would make it up. To me, and to Stewart!" He paced the softly moving deck. "She seemed to have no sense of time anymore. It was all a few years, a few days. Me and Stewart all in the same time, as if we were the same man."

"In a way I think you were," Beckett said. "Hansen and all the others she didn't marry were the same man. Only it looks like Hansen may have been one man too much. Hansen, the cube house brawl, and Stewart, the last straw."

"The last—?" McKay breathed deeply. "You think she's going to—?" He couldn't seem to finish it.

"Did you know she tried suicide twice? Once before she married you, once a few years after she divorced you."

McKay stopped pacing. He turned to Beckett as if trying to determine if Beckett knew what he had said, was sure.

"No, I didn't know. My God, if I'd known I might have done things differently."

McKay walked forward into the bow of the long sloop. Beckett followed him. McKay stood in the curve of the bow rail and looked out over the bowsprit at the open sea beyond the breakwater in the afternoon sun. His voice as distant as the sea.

"Most of us marry the first one who'll marry us, who seems to fit our needs. We don't examine those needs to be sure they are real." McKay's eyes followed a line of black-suited surfers in the far distance near the beach. "We marry for sex and life-style—the life-style we've been told we ought to have. Maybe the sex is bad or the life-style is wrong. We break up without knowing really why, or go on, inadequate to the end.

"I felt she was always in a contest with me, a war, to be better than I was at everything. I suppose it was the same with Stewart, but he was a gentler man, more sure of himself, so he lasted longer.

"We only had Bill. We began in a double bed. After Bill was born she wanted twin beds. I hated it, but I lived with it. Then she wanted separate bedrooms, and that I wouldn't live with. I suppose it was the same for Stewart: double bed, twin beds, separate rooms, and finally out of the house into that room over the garage. Yet she *needed* love. At the end she began—"

"Having affairs," Beckett said. "With pickups, any-one."

McKay nodded. "Why?"

"She wants life to be different," Beckett said. "She wants herself to be different, but she can't hide from life."

"I suppose I should thank her. She never told me her own inner troubles, made it easy for me to walk away."

"She couldn't do anything else," Beckett said.

"No," McKay said. He turned from the distant sea. "I guess we're all pushed by forces inside we don't even know are there. Like any animal, we act in ignorance of our motives, of what drives us. It seems it *is* in our stars that we are underlings, you know? The stars we have inside, the forces that shaped us."

190

He became silent in the low sunlight. Beckett waited.

McKay said, "You think she killed Stewart. You think she was the woman I saw at the garage that night. You think she killed Spira because he had found out."

"Where did you follow her? Where did you lose her?"

"She drove to a house on Olive Street, number twenty-seven. Then she went uptown. I lost her at a red light on Cota Street."

"Stay here," Beckett said. "You understand?"

*

John Perkins sat alone in his office.

The sunlight outside his windows had changed from the silver of morning to the gold of afternoon to the blue shadows of dusk while he had sat there doing nothing, like a silent mourner at some long-ago old-country funeral.

The bottle he had gone to buy and bring back somewhere between the silver and the gold was half empty.

He sat at his drawing table, the plans of the cube house spread out before him.

He was not drunk.

He was no longer drinking.

He only sat, the blue shadows of dusk turning into a shadowless darkness outside, and let his fingers rest on the outlines of the dream house that had become a reality on a springlike day so many months ago.

A reality and a nightmare.

*

Number 27 Olive Street was a frame bungalow with a postage stamp front lawn in an area of older houses near the harbor. Beckett parked up the street and walked slowly back. A blue Datsun stood in the driveway in the darkness.

Beckett walked around the house. The tiny backyard was

191

empty, and there was no sign of Barbara Stewart's Nova. The windows of the little house were open, the shades up, and some laundry and bathing suits hung on the line in the night. Beckett returned to the front door, rang. And rang again.

No one answered. No one moved inside. In the silence he became aware of a radio playing somewhere inside. The front door was locked. He went to the rear. The back door was locked.

Through the open kitchen window he saw the remains of a meal still on the kitchen table. A large cat sat in another open window watching Beckett through the screen. As he watched, it clawed at the screen, its eyes questioning him.

"Hey, you want the Krankls?"

A dark-skinned man leaned out an open window of the next house. Beckett walked to the fence.

"Oscar Krankl?" he said. "Yes, you know where they are?"

"Went off in that big cruiser," the man said, envious. "Must of cost twenty-five, thirty thousand. A G.M. cruiser, you know? Sleeps a whole family, got a kitchen 'n living room, and you drive it like a car. Sweet."

"A mobile-home cruiser?"

"Yep. Wish I could pick up that kind of cash. Those government guys got the angles, right? Must of been moon-lighting, the nights he works."

"When did they leave?"

"Maybe two o'clock, around there. I give 'em a wave, only I guess Krankl didn't see me. Headed for the freeway north."

Beckett looked back at the silent bungalow. The cat mewed behind the screen. Beckett walked to the window, broke the screen, and pulled the metal cloth open. The cat backed away, watched from inside the kitchen. As Beckett went to his car, the cat leaped out and vanished into the night.

He drove to the first telephone booth. He called Tucker.

"It's coming together, Charley. Get to Hoag, tell him to put out an all-state call to pick up a General Motors mobile cruiser registered to Oscar Krankl, Twenty-seven Olive Street."

"Oscar Krankl?"

"Yeh. It's headed north probably, but tell Hoag to alert the CHP in all directions. He can get the license from DMV in Sacramento, or maybe someone in Krankl's office knows where he bought it and can give us the license. Tell Hoag urgent."

Beckett drove straight to the Hansen Realty office in its side-street bungalow. The office was dark, no one answered. He drove south to the big old fake Tudor house on the way to Cuyama Beach. Ann Hansen stared at him stonily.

"Is Barbara Stewart here? Has she been?"

"No," Ann Hansen said. "She hasn't and she won't."

"Won't?"

"We talked it out, came to a détente."

"Where's Hansen?"

The big real estate man appeared behind his wife. He was in his shirt sleeves, looked haggard behind the athletic manner. Ann Hansen walked away into the house.

"Have you seen Barbara Stewart?" Beckett said. "Or heard from her?"

"No, and I'm worried as hell." Hansen glanced behind him. His wife wasn't in sight now. "Come into the den."

Hansen closed the door. "I haven't seen her for three days. We had business, she didn't show. At least three sales are hanging. I heard you were looking, hoped you had her."

"I don't. No ideas where she is or why?"

"Not a glimmer, except . . . She hasn't been herself, you know? I mean, since Stewart. Sure, it was a shock, but to leave three sales hanging?" Hansen bit a fingernail. It was about the last he had long enough to bite. "I've got this feeling it's more than just Stewart, you know?"

Beckett said, "Guilt?"

"You too?" Hansen worried the nail, brushed the shard from his lip. "But, Christ, not Barbara! She was with me when Stewart died, and why would she kill George Spira?"

"You're sure she was with you all that night?"

Hansen looked away. "After I picked her up."

"And that was around midnight?"

Hansen studied a wall. "Maybe a little later. Look, she couldn't have killed Spira! A gun? She—"

Beckett took out the gray button. "I found this on the floor of Spira's car."

Hansen went white. Literally. "My God!" He stared at the button. "Does . . . does she know you have that? Know you're after her?"

"I don't know, maybe. People could have told her. Why? You think she'll do something? Suicide? Has she tried that before?"

Hansen nodded, his face miserable. "We've got to find her. She must be sick, you know? Maybe the office? Or that McKay and his boat? Maybe her son?"

"I've been to your office and to McKay. Her son says he hasn't seen her. Anyway, he's staying at her house."

"Have you tried the house?"

"Not today. Maybe we should."

"I'll get my car, follow you!"

Hansen ran out of the house. Beckett walked.

*

Alone in the kitchen of the cube house, Cathy Perkins heard the sound out in the night again. As if someone were

194

walking in the thick brush at the edge of the access road. She had heard no car.

In the living room the lights of the city below seemed a thousand miles away as she stood listening.

The sound came again. Closer to the house. Then stopped. There was no brush or bushes near the house.

She stood at the front door. She opened it.

"John? John! Is that you, John?"

A shadow moved at the corner of the house.

"Who is it? Who's out there?"

There was no answer.

24

The lighted windows of the big white house in Cuyama Beach seemed to flicker through the trees that blew in a rising sea wind. Phil Hansen got to the door first. Grace Mackay peered out into the night past the real estate man.

"Mr. Hansen! Is that Barbara with . . . Oh, Mr. Beckett."

"She's not here?" Hansen said.

"No. I thought perhaps she was with you. I mean—"

Beckett said, "Can we come in?"

"Oh, yes, please do."

She followed them into the large, pleasant living room with its solid old furniture. There was no sign of anyone else in the big house. The children's voices came from somewhere upstairs. Muted children's voices, well trained, and Beckett realized that he had never seen the Mackay children, or found them downstairs.

"Your husband isn't home either?" Beckett asked.

"No, he has some late work."

Hansen said, "You were home all day?"

196

"Oh, no. The children are taking private lessons while we're here, Bill always insists on that. He says they learn more in a few weeks that way than in a year in public school. I walk on the beach while they're at lessons. I collect shells. Then I do the marketing, run errands. I keep busy." She smiled.

"Then you've been out most of the day?" Beckett said.

"Yes. I got home about five-thirty."

"Can we look at her room?"

"Why, I never thought of that! She could have come home while I was out, and be up there now. Asleep, perhaps!"

They went up to the second-floor master bedroom. Barbara Stewart wasn't there.

The bed was unused, there was no sign of anyone having been in the bathroom. Grace Mackay and Hansen found no trace of her in the other bedrooms. A thin film of dust covered everything on her bed table and writing desk. On the top sheet of a pad of monogrammed note paper she had written a note to remind herself to call Ann Hansen. It was dated five days ago.

They went downstairs.

"If she comes home," Beckett said, "call me right away."

"And me," Hansen said.

As they returned to their cars, Grace Mackay stood in the open doorway watching them as if she suddenly didn't want to be alone. Beckett didn't get into his car. He stood in the light from the house and looked toward the garage.

"Mrs. Mackay," he said, "did you close the garage door?"

"Close?" She came out and looked. "No, we don't use the garage. There's only room for the Cadillac and the Nova."

197

"It was open two nights ago, after Mrs. Stewart had gone."

"Maybe Mackay closed it," Hansen said.

"Maybe," Beckett said as he walked toward the garage.

Grace Mackay and Hansen came behind him. The main door was locked. Beckett peered inside through the small window in the door. He started around the side.

"The Nova's in there," he said.

The side door was unlocked. Beckett turned on the light inside. Barbara Stewart sat in the front seat behind the wheel. She seemed to be watching them through the windshield.

"Barbara?" Hansen said.

Beckett walked around to the driver's side. The left side of her head was gone, a black hole of dried blood. The window was splattered with blood and bone, shattered by the bullet.

"Oh my God!" Hansen said.

The big real estate man leaned against the garage wall, his head down, his chest and stomach heaving but nothing coming out. Grace Mackay covered her mouth, turned away.

Beckett opened the Nova door. She was dead, had been for perhaps four hours or so, the body cold and her jaw and neck already stiff with rigor. The big Colt .45-caliber automatic lay on the floor under her dangling right hand. There were small smears of oil on her hand.

The note lay on the floor of the passenger side. There was no blood on it. A simple note on a sheet of her own note paper, written in blue ink. *"I think of this as a simple act of going home, I am sorry if it will cause anyone pain. I feel no pain, only relief to leave this dirt, greed and filth we call life. It is peaceful, I am happy. Forgive me, Barbara."*

"Is it her handwriting?" Beckett asked.

Hansen nodded.

198

"I think so," Grace Mackay said. She stared at Barbara Stewart now. "Why? I don't understand."

"She must have killed Stewart," Hansen said, his voice dull. "And Spira too."

"It looks like the gun that killed Spira all right," Beckett said. "Ballistics will check, but I'd bet on it. All right, Hansen, now tell me the real story of that night."

"She called me, asked me to come right over, said hurry." Hansen said. "I came. She was standing behind the garage. She was all shook up, asked me to take her to the office. I did. I didn't know about Stewart until Mackay told me next morning."

"No one else was around?"

"I don't know, I was too busy helping her to my car. I thought maybe I saw someone way off in the trees in front of the house, but I wasn't sure. I didn't know about Stewart! When I found out, I couldn't turn her in! She didn't remember, but was ready to confess anyway, and I couldn't let her." He stared at the dead woman in the car. "Maybe I should have."

"Maybe you should have," Beckett said. "Go up above and call Hoag. You better wait in the house, Mrs. Mackay."

Alone, he examined the car again. He found nothing. He poked carefully through her handbag with the tip of his pen. He studied the note on the floor. There was a sag to his heavy shoulders, defeat in his impassive blue eyes.

Hansen ran back into the garage.

"They're coming, but not Hoag! He's out at the cube house, it's on fire! I've got to go out there."

"I'll wait for Hoag's men, and come after you."

The deputies arrived in fifteen minutes. Beckett showed them the note, told them there was another note in her room for comparison. He told them to take the note and the gun to the lab for analysis. Then he hurried out to follow Hansen to the cube house.

*

There were no fire engines on the access road as Beckett turned off the highway, and when he crested the rise he saw the flames against the dark sky in the distance. Houses burned on the slopes of Mar Vista like the aftermath of a shelling in the war. Isolated houses burning fiercely the way they had in Alsace as he had advanced toward the Germans so long ago. And beyond the burning houses the sea wind pushed the fire on through the brush as the firemen fought to stem the spread and save Mar Vista.

Beckett parked on the access road, walked across the charred brush toward the cube house. There was no fire here now, no engines, no battle. A silence as in a captured village after the war has moved on.

But the cube house was gone.

A still-smoldering skeleton on its small hill. Next door the Bowman ranch house was untouched. Someone walked around it with a flashlight. Beyond that Colonel Hillock's house still burned, giving off a fierce light. All fires were capricious.

Beckett saw that nothing had burned on the highway, the seaward side of the cube house. A knot of shadowy people had gathered near the skeleton of the cube house. In the sporadic flares of light he saw Sheriff Hoag with some of his men. Phil Hansen was there, and Colonel Hillock and his wife. And the magazine man, Burt Tarcher. That was all.

"The cube house first?" Beckett said to Hoag.

"Set deliberately," Hoag said. His bland face was blackened and angry. "The Chief found gasoline, matches, charred cloth. The wind whipped it into the brush, of course. It skipped the Bowmans, got Hillock, and went on up and over. Lucky for all of us it's a sea wind away from

200

town, and luckier for Mar Vista it's a cool wind. They've about got it stopped up ahead."

"Starting a fire in brush country, Jesus!" Hansen said.

"Well," Colonel Hillock said, "I guess I don't have to sell after all, do I, Hansen? Take the insurance and run."

"You were selling your house?" Beckett said.

"I think I've had about enough of real estate." Hillock hadn't looked toward his burning house since Beckett had arrived, he didn't look now. "I'm a soldier, not a businessman. Maybe I can still get some civilian work with the service." He glanced at his wife. She hadn't stopped staring at the bright shadow of their burning house. "Or a private job where my training will fit. Maybe overseas. Anywhere."

"Anywhere," Patricia Hillock said. "Home is matched luggage."

"But not right away," Beckett said. "We've got three deaths, and now arson."

"Three?" Patricia Hillock said.

Beckett told them about Barbara Stewart.

"Poor woman," Patricia Hillock said.

"Arson?" Hillock said. "You think someone set this fire?"

"Someone who really hated that house," Hoag said. "Did you have anything to do with hiring Bill Mackay, Colonel?"

"Nothing!" Hillock snapped. "And I told Bowman not to."

"He didn't listen," Hoag said.

Angry voices on the access road made them all turn. Their faces and eyes seemed to move in and out of darkness as the burning houses and the distant brush-flames flickered the night. On the road two deputies were blocking a man trying to come toward the cube house ruin. ". . . *my wife . . . house . . .*"

"Let him through!" Hoag called.

John Perkins came running up through the blackened brush. He didn't even look at the skeleton of his dream house.

"Where's my wife?"

"Over there," Hoag said.

He pointed to the front lawn of the Bowman house, a miraculous island in the sea of black. Three vague shadows stood over something on the ground. Hoag and Perkins walked toward the group. The others drifted after them, a lethargy hanging over them as the light of the burning houses died, and the brush began to subside in the distance as the firemen gained control. The three people standing on the lawn were two deputies and Cathy Perkins. The man seated on the ground was Maxwell Bowman.

"I'm sorry, Cath," Perkins said. "I had no call to judge you for doing what you felt you had to."

"Perhaps I was wrong," Cathy said. "It all seems so futile now, such a waste. I'll give the money back."

Burt Tarcher said, "Hell no, a deal's a deal. Besides, we get one big story out of it—what the fear of anything different, the fear of change, can do to people. Hell, it might even be a better story this way, fire and murder because someone didn't want to be just like everyone else, eh? And if you rebuild it and go on, I'll be back."

"Rebuild it?" Now Perkins looked at the charred ruin, at the open space where the wall had been and the lights of the city clear below. "I don't know. Is it worth it?"

"It's important that a person be able to build his own house where he wants it," Cathy said. "His own dream."

"Maybe a house is a lousy dream," Perkins said. "Maybe we've been too narrow, too selfish. Careers,

202

houses, our own enjoyment. Maybe people count more. A family?''

Cathy smiled, ''We'll talk about it.''

Perkins smiled, ''Yeh, we'll talk.''

They walked away. Not toward the skeleton of the cube house, but toward the access road where Perkins had left his car. Beckett watched them go. Sheriff Hoag looked down at Maxwell Bowman.

''He was here when we arrived,'' Hoag said, watched the old man seated on the lawn with his head down. ''With Cathy Perkins. He'd helped her get a few things from the house, tried to fight it spreading to the brush. There were four of them: Mackay and his two buddies, and Bowman.''

Bowman looked up, his eyes bloodshot in a blackened face. He looked at all of them as if for some answer. ''They started it, Bill Mackay and his two goons, and I helped them. Mrs. Perkins heard us, came out. Mackay hadn't even checked to see if she was here, the stupid fool! I couldn't take it anymore. I went to help her. Mackay tried to stop me, but other people were coming already, we could hear sirens. The two goons ran off. Mackay just stood there for a while watching me. Then he left. He just walked away. I guess he knew I'd tell it all.''

''You're in a lot of trouble, Bowman,'' Hoag said.

Bowman wasn't listening. He was staring toward his own house with its lights alone in the night like a ship far out on a dark ocean. Someone still walked around the house with a flashlight. It was Estelle Bowman out in the night examining her flowers, making sure they were all safe.

''At least she still has the house,'' Bowman said. ''They didn't destroy it with their damned blank wall!''

''You'll be okay, Bowman,'' Burt Tarcher said. ''You'll tell it all, apologize, and at your age they'll let you off easy.''

Beckett said to Hoag, "Have you picked up Mackay?"

"Not yet. No hurry. The roads are all covered."

"He'll go to his family, get them safe."

"He won't get far," Hoag said.

"I want him now," Beckett said. "Barbara Stewart didn't kill herself."

25

Grace Mackay said, "Bill! Barbara's dead! She shot herself!"

Mackay went on packing the suitcase in the upstairs bedroom of the big house. "I'm sorry about that, but we don't have much time. I'll probably be gone at least a couple of years—"

"Don't you care? Oh, Bill!"

"Care?" Mackay stopped packing, looked up at her. "I care, but there's no point getting sentimental, that's useless and weak. She was suicidal. I always suspected something was wrong with her, I never knew what. Maybe she's better off now."

Grace stood silent. Mackay went on packing.

"Are the kids ready?" he said.

She nodded. He closed the suitcase, stood up. "You know where my papers are, and the money. Eller will get a lawyer, he owes me that. He owes me money too, see that you get it. If things get difficult, our friends will help you somehow."

"Perhaps, when you explain, they'll—?"

"I won't beg and I won't deal!" Mackay said fiercely. "It had to be done, most of them know that, but they won't stand up like men. They'll cry and throw me to the wolves. Maybe I deserve it. I should have known Bowman would crack. We'd never have been identified otherwise. No, I failed, Grace."

"Will they arrest Mr. Bowman too?"

"A slap," Mackay said. "They better keep him away from me or I'll kill him!"

"Bill!"

He faced her. "I have no regrets. I consider it my duty. I do my duty, make the children understand that."

"Yes, Bill."

"Okay, let's go." He picked up the three suitcases. "With any luck it won't matter, we'll still beat them."

*

The big white house was dark as Beckett and Hoag turned into the driveway. Nothing moved in the night.

"Where are your deputies?" Beckett said as they got out of their cars in the silence under the trees.

"There should be one at the garage anyway," Hoag said. He sent the two men with him to look in the garage.

Beckett led the way into the house. No one was there.

"Their stuff is gone," Beckett said.

The deputies shouted from the garage. Beckett and Hoag ran out and across the yard under the silent trees. There were three deputies at the garage. The third one had blood on his head, was still taking the rope off his legs.

"He jumped me! The doc had taken her body, the lab guys took the note and gun, and I was guarding the scene when Mackay jumped me!"

"How long ago?" Hoag barked.

"Maybe twenty minutes." The deputy rubbed at his head.

"Which way did they go?" Beckett asked.

"North, I'm pretty sure."

"Sacramento?" Hoag suggested.

Beckett thought. "Mexico would be his best bet, but that's south. Only if I know Mackay he'd have had some plan of escape."

"We've got all the ways out blocked."

"All?" Beckett said. "What about by sea?"

"No!" Hoag swore. "The *Paloma?*"

They drove north and through Fremont to the marina. The forest of boats rocked in their docks in the night. The *Paloma* was still there. The children played silently on the deck. Hoag stationed one man on the pier, sent the others forward to watch the hatches. Beckett called down into the lighted cabin.

"Mackay? Hoag's men are all around. Come on out."

There was a pause. Then Mackay's voice called up.

"You come on down."

Hoag motioned his men down the forward hatches. He and Beckett went down the main companionway. Tom McKay stood in the cabin with his back to them. Grace Mackay sat on a bench. Bill Mackay faced his father, a gun in his hand.

"My men are behind you," Hoag said. "Put the gun down."

Mackay's eyes seemed to flare for an instant. Then he laid the gun on the cabin table. "Call Senator Eller, I want a lawyer."

Tom McKay spoke without turning or taking his eyes off his son. "He wanted me to say he'd been here all night. I refused. He told me to sail him to Mexico. I said no. He took out that gun. He's not my son. He's a brainless savage."

"Run, old man," Mackay said. "Hide from reality."

207

Tom McKay sat down at the cabin table. "He told me about Barbara. I'm sorry. Perhaps if—?" He didn't finish. "So it's all over?"

"Not quite," Beckett said. "Mackay didn't tell us about one thing he did in Stewart's room that morning."

Tom McKay was up. "You mean he—!"

"No," Beckett said, "he didn't kill Stewart, but he's known from the start who did. Right, Mackay?"

Bill Mackay shrugged.

"How did he know?" Hoag said. "What did he do?"

"He took Stewart's keys from the upstairs bureau, and put them into the Cadillac."

Mackay laughed. "Did I do that? Prove it."

"I won't have to, nothing else makes sense," Beckett said. He turned to Hoag. "There were only two sets of keys. Barbara had hers with her, so if Stewart's had been on the bureau we'd have known she killed him. Mackay guessed what had happened when he saw no keys in the Caddy. But he saw a chance to cover for Barbara and play his own game too. He wanted to keep the cube house pot boiling, make it an even bigger issue, and try to accuse the Perkinses of murder. So he put Stewart's keys in the Caddy, and went to work both framing the Perkinses and scaring them to make them give up."

"Does it matter?" Tom McKay said. "She killed Stewart."

"She killed him, but it wasn't murder. It was an accident. She went to that garage to kill herself."

Beckett sat on the edge of the cabin table, his leg swinging. He looked down at Mackay's gun. "She had a history of suicide. A woman in conflict with the world and herself. Married twice, but never really married. When she was twelve or so her father gave her a private room with a private bathroom, her own little world. Private and isolated. She never really liked life anywhere else, and her whole adult life became a subconscious drive to return to that special, private room. To her solitary room, her kingdom, and eventually to untouched peace."

No one spoke, but Grace Mackay wiped at her eyes. A sadness on her face, even an understanding.

"Suicide," Beckett said. "Not always, but when something happened to trigger a self-disgust so intense she couldn't go on living with herself. McKay and Judy Muldahr both told how she was distraught, spaced out, *before* Stewart died. She visited McKay for the first time in twenty years. She was retracing her life just as she did later, putting it in order, and she intended to kill herself that night. But something happened, and she didn't die. But Stewart did. By accident."

Hoag said, "What happened that saved her?"

"Call in," Beckett said. "See if they've got Krankl."

Hoag went up on deck. In the cabin they waited. Beckett continued to swing his leg. He watched Bill Mackay.

"If you hadn't used Stewart's death for your own ends, Mackay, she might still be alive. Spira would be."

"I did what had to be done," Mackay said. "Someday even you might wake up, see the truth, thank me."

"Does your wife thank you?" Beckett said.

Grace Mackay said, "My husband's kind of man is the hope of our country, Mr. Beckett. Eventually people will see that. I can wait as long as I must, like a soldier's wife. When he comes home, I'll be there."

"Yeh," Beckett said.

Hoag returned. "They picked up Krankl and his family all the way up in Pismo Beach. He's in my office in San Vicente."

"I'll talk to him on your radio," Beckett said.

The deputies brought Bill Mackay to the sheriff's car.

Grace Mackay and the children would go back to the house in Cuyama Beach. It was theirs now. Tom McKay stood alone on the dark deck of the *Paloma*. It was his home.

*

Paul Hansen opened the door of the fake Tudor house in south Fremont. His face was still smudged from the fire. He had a whisky in his hand. He tried to smile. He couldn't.

Ann Hansen sat in the shabby living room as Hoag and Beckett came in. Two deputies waited in the doorway with Mackay.

"Barbara Stewart didn't call you that night," Beckett said to the big real estate man, "you called her. Tom McKay heard the phone ringing a long time. When you got no answer you were worried and went to the house. You heard the Cadillac running in the garage, and found her in it. You got her out into the weeds where that depression was. It took time to revive her, maybe half an hour, and you left the car running. Later you shut it off, took her keys—you wanted no possible evidence of a suicide try. By then Stewart was dead upstairs, but you didn't know that until Bill Mackay came to your office and told both of you."

Hansen's voice was cracked and hoarse. "Why would I do all that? You're wrong."

"For the same reason the cube house mess had you so worried," Beckett said. "Oscar Krankl told us the whole scheme."

"Scheme?" Ann Hansen said, sat up. "What scheme?"

"A nice little swindle," Hoag said. "Krankl's a Federal Housing Authority appraiser. Hansen and Barbara Stewart bought falling-apart houses cheap, painted over the ruin, and Krankl blew up the appraised value for FHA mortgage guarantee. That way they could sell them for very low payments, even at the inflated price, to marginal buyers who could never get a house any other way and didn't ask questions."

210

"The house falls apart," Beckett said, "the buyer can't repair it *and* make payments, the mortgage is foreclosed, and the government picks it up. The swindlers make a fat profit, the buyer loses cash *and* house, the government owns a wreck."

Hansen looked at his wife. His hollow eyes pleaded.

"But," Beckett said, "he became scared that the cube house furor would draw attention to his business so he asked Barbara to try to get Stewart to settle it quickly and quietly. She did—and then the whole mess suddenly made her sick. She was in a dirty deal, trying to hide it, while Stewart was defending right and principle. With all the rest of her guilt and self-hate it triggered another suicide try. Only Hansen saved her because he knew a suicide would bring it all out for sure."

"No," Hansen said. "She killed Stewart. Her deal too. Mackay didn't switch keys. Tell them, Mackay."

"No use," Beckett said. "Krankl already told us that Spira had discovered the swindles, was going to meet you and Barbara. Barbara didn't have that Colt. She was wearing her gray suit the first night, probably lost the button in your office and you pocketed it without thinking. She couldn't really have dragged Spira up those stairs, but you could, and you did. A panicky try to confuse things."

"She killed Stewart," Hansen said as if Beckett had never spoken. "She killed Spira and herself. You saw the note."

"Yeh," Beckett said. "In her bedroom tonight there was dust on her memo pad. It's a gummed pad, there was a note on top five days old. She couldn't have written the suicide note *after* that note. No, it was written for her *first* suicide. You took it with you the first night, and planted it tonight!"

Hansen looked at his whisky. "She had the paper in her handbag! She wrote the note in the car!"

Beckett shook his head. "There was no pen in her bag, Hansen. No pen in the car or garage. The lab will prove the note was written a week ago. No one in Fremont knew she was suicidal except you and Bill Mackay because of the first night. Mackay had no motive to kill her, but you did. She told Tom McKay she was going to 'clean it up, balance the books.' She told Krankl she was going to confess, and she told you too. Krankl ran, but you didn't. She was going to kill herself this time too, but she was going to expose it all first. You'd killed Spira to cover up. So you killed her too, faked the suicide with the old note."

Hoag nodded to his deputies. They moved toward Hansen. His glass hit the floor and smashed, and he held a gun.

He waved the gun. "Get away! Don't come near me!"

"Put it down," Hoag said. "You've got nowhere to go."

"No!" The gun moved wildly. "I . . . nowhere to—?"

He turned and ran into the next room. The door closed. Hoag started after him.

"No," Beckett said. He watched the closed door, waited.

They all waited. Ann Hansen was on her feet. Bill Mackay's eyes glistened and his lips moved urgently.

The whole shabby house seemed to listen, to wait. There was only silence.

The door opened again. Hansen came out. He put the pistol on a table. He sat down.

"Shit," Mackay said, scornful.

Ann Hansen cried, "Give me the gun! I'll do it! No damned money for lawyers! What do I do now? What the hell do I do? Give it to me, damn him!"

A deputy restrained her. Hoag picked up the gun. Hansen sat staring ahead at nothing, his big hands clasped between his knees, hunched forward.

His voice came from nowhere. "They had to build that

nightmare house. They had to stir up the whole town. She had to fall apart. All I asked her to do was keep it quiet, try to calm it all down, try to get Stewart to compromise, put a little squeeze on him to settle out of court." He looked up, blinked, his eyes puzzled. "Dirty, she said, all of us. All stink and filth. Stewart was a good man, honest, strong, and we were rotten. *She* was the worst, she hated herself."

Outrage came into his monotonous voice in the room. "She had to try to kill herself! It would have brought everyone down on us. I stopped her, got her out, and then Stewart was dead! Spira had to snoop around! She had to tell! *Tell!* After I'd had to . . . stop Spira. She'd tried to kill herself once, I had the note, it was so easy."

"It always is," Beckett said.

Hoag motioned to his men.

"Why?" Hansen said. He looked up at all of them. "No one would have known, no one would have cared. A few thousand bucks the government would never even miss, no one hurt. Half the businesses in the country live off the government, I just wanted my share. A few dollars. No one would have been hurt."

Beckett said, "What about the poor people you sold those houses to? All they wanted was a home, a miracle. You took what little they had and left them with nothing!"

"Where were they going?" Hansen said. "What were they ever going to have? Nothing! Losers, bums! I had a business, all I needed was a chance and I'd be big. Those houses were my chance, you know? My chance!"

Hansen began to cry. Ann Hansen sat alone in a corner. Bill Mackay stood disgusted. The deputies took Hansen out. Hoag and Beckett took Mackay. In the night the two police cars drove north to Fremont and then east toward San Vicente.

"The goddamn fool," Hoag said. "For what? A couple of

213

years in Chino at the worst. A fine."

"He wanted the money," Beckett said. "It happens every day somewhere. But this time Perkins had to build his dream house in a place where different dreams aren't wanted, and Barbara Stewart was a woman who didn't like the world the way it is, lived too close to death."

"I'm sorry about how I treated Charley Tucker," Hoag said.

"I'm sorry I didn't tell you about the button and what I was doing," Beckett said.

They drove on to San Vicente and the courthouse.